My Life in Pink & Green

AMULET BOOKS

NEW YORK

The Library of Congress has cataloged the hardcover edition of this book as follows:

Greenwald, Lisa.
My life in pink and green / by Lisa Greenwald.
p. cm.
Summary: When the family's drugstore is failing, seventh grader Lucy uses her problem-solving talents
to come up with a solution that might resuscitate the business, along with helping the environment.
ISBN 978-0-8109-8352-6 (alk. paper)
[1. Family problems—Fiction. 2. Mothers and daughters—Fiction. 3. Cosmetics—Fiction.
4. Green movement—Fiction.] I. Title.

PZ7.G85199My 2009
[Fic]—dc22
2008025577

Paperback ISBN 978-0-8109-8587-2

Orginally published in hardcover by Amulet Books in 2009

Text copyright © 2009 Lisa Greenwald

Book design by Chad W. Beckerman

Laura Mercier epigraphs reprinted with permission of Atria Books, a Division of Simon & Schuster, Inc.,
from *The New Beauty Secrets: Your Ultimate Guide to a Flawless Face* by Laura Mercier.
Copyright © 2006 by Gurwitch Products, LLC.

ABRAMS
THE ART OF BOOKS SINCE 1949
115 West 18th Street
New York, NY 10011
www.abramsbooks.com

For Dare

Beauty tip: Putting cold cucumbers on your
eyes can reduce puffiness and relieve stress.

Things can always be worse. That's what
Grandma says, anyway, whenever something really bad
happens. I've always thought that was a pretty good way to
look at life. But lately I'm not so sure, because I don't think
things can really get any worse.

It's Friday afternoon—a time when most normal seventh-
grade girls would be at a friend's house or maybe the mall or
even the movies.

But where am I?

The pharmacy.

And what am I doing?

Opening mail.

When I'm at the pharmacy after school, it's my job to open
the mail. I do it first thing so that I have the rest of the time
free. But it's not like there's so much for me to do the rest of

the time. It's not like if I don't open the mail first thing, I won't have time to do it later. I just don't like to have things hanging over my head.

I bet most kids my age would find opening the mail to be the most boring thing in the world. And sometimes it is. But it's also kind of comforting. I like coming to the pharmacy straight from school and having my snack in the back office.

It's nice to know you always have a place to go.

Besides, I don't usually read the mail; I just open it and put it in a neat pile. But today big, bold, black letters catch my eye: THREE DELINQUENT MORTGAGE PAYMENTS. My throat starts to feel like it's getting tighter and tighter, almost like it's closing up. And my heart starts beating fast and furious, when it was beating calmly just a second ago.

THREE DELINQUENT MORTGAGE PAYMENTS. What does that mean? That we haven't paid the mortgage for three months? Or that the payments weren't enough?

The next sentence: YOU ARE IN DANGER OF FORECLOSURE.

We get a lot of mail at the pharmacy because we get all of the business mail, obviously, and all of our regular mail too. The pharmacy is like our second home. Lately I'm beginning to think we spend more time there than at our real house.

"Jane!" Grandma calls. I see her coming into the office, and I try to put the letter under the stack of regular mail, but I'm not quick enough. Grandma hasn't even said hi to me yet and already she's upset. "Jane Scarlett Desberg!"

Even though my mom's forty, my grandma still uses her whole name when she's angry at her.

"Ma, what?" My mom comes into the office, her cleaning apron only half on. She was in the middle of dusting and reorganizing her favorite section of the store—the magazine area. Old Mill Pharmacy doesn't just carry the usual magazines like *People* and *Glamour* and *Time.* We have those, but we also carry magazines that are hard to find on the average drugstore news rack, like the *Nation* and the *Progressive.*

My mom's a huge reader. She'll read anything she can get her hands on, and especially stuff about people making a difference or taking a stand on complicated issues. She doesn't just accept situations as they are—she's always questioning things, so she likes to read magazines and newspapers that reflect that state of mind.

She's one of those people who truly believe one person can change the world.

"'Three delinquent mortgage payments'—that's what!" Grandma shoves the letter in front of my mom's nose. "'In danger of foreclosure'! Can you please explain?"

My mom rolls her eyes and fastens her apron around her waist, admiring herself in the office's full-length mirror. "Oh, Ma. They always say that. We'll pay. Don't worry. I've been putting off our last few payments to save up for the Small Businesses, Big World conference I told you about. We need to do more than just fill prescriptions. Our business can make a difference in the world. We just need to find out what we can do."

Grandma's face falls. The tension in the room seems to be expanding like a balloon that's about to pop. This is my time to walk away. "I'm going to straighten up the toy section!" I say, more cheerfully than I'd normally say it.

But instead of straightening, I close the door and wait outside the office so that I can eavesdrop. I need to find out what *foreclosure* means.

I make fake walking sounds so that Mom and Grandma think I'm far enough away that I won't be able to hear them, and then I scooch down toward the floor and gently press my ear against the wooden door.

"Jane, time to come out of your save-the-world daze, sweetheart," Grandma says. "We don't have enough money to save the world. We need to save this pharmacy. You have two children to support. And frankly, I'm sick of having to tell you this."

"Ma, relax," Mom says, acting like she has everything under control. There's a long silence, and I'm wondering if the conversation's over and if I really should go and clean the toy section.

"We're sitting down tonight with all of the bills," Grandma says, sounding calmer now. "And I'm letting Tory and Charise go. I have to. I don't have a choice."

Tory and Charise have been working at the pharmacy for as long as I can remember. Tory does all of the loading and unloading of boxes and stocking of the shelves. And Charise makes sure the pharmacy's spick-and-span and helps out behind the counter. She always tells me stories about the old days, when people would have to wait in line for sodas and snacks and stuff. I even remember when Grandpa was alive and so many of the kids in our neighborhood would hang out at the store, having snacks at the counter after school. Sometimes Grandpa would even help them with their homework.

It's not like that anymore. Not at all.

Nowadays, people will occasionally come in for a soda, but they're usually high school kids who are going to the movies next door and don't want to pay movie-theater prices. No one ever orders items from the grill; Grandma barely even turns it on anymore. Things have changed a lot, and not in a good way. I wish there was a way to go back to the way they used to be.

I especially feel bad for Tory and Charise. I know they need the money. And I know Grandma would never let them go if she didn't have to.

That's how I know things are bad.

Business tip: Follow up with new clients,
but make sure to stay in touch with old ones too.

When I tell my sister that Grandma has just laid off Tory and Charise, she says what she always says: "I'm coming home. That's it. There's no reason why I need to be at some fancy-pants private school when you're all struggling. I'll come home, go to UConn, and that'll be that."

"Claudia," I say in my groany voice. "No one expects you to do that."

"Put Mom on the phone," Claudia insists. So I walk downstairs and hand Mom the cordless. She's making chicken and her famous Spanish rice, and I hate, hate, hate Spanish rice more than anything in the world. She makes it extra spicy with jalapeños, and the recipe doesn't even call for that.

I can only hear my mom's end of the conversation, and all she's saying is, "No, that won't be necessary," and "Honey, this doesn't concern you," and finally "I hope you've been eating only organic meat, because you know how they are treating animals these days."

Finally, she hangs up. She pushes her blonde spiral curls behind her ears. "Lucy, go wash up. And call Grandma at the pharmacy and tell her dinner will be ready in five minutes. Either she gets here in time, or we eat without her."

It's already eight thirty and we haven't even eaten dinner yet. That isn't normal. Well, it's normal for us, but not normal for normal people. But even though my mom threatens to eat without Grandma, I know we won't. We always eat together as a family. As Grandma always says, "A family that eats together, stays together."

Grandma gets home just in time, and she puts the chicken cutlets on a platter while Mom serves the rice.

At first we're all quiet because we're so busy eating.

"Delicious rice, Jane," Grandma says after a few minutes. "It gets better each time you make it. The sautéed onions are perfect." I know this is just a simple compliment, but it's a relief to hear, considering how much Grandma and Mom have been fighting lately.

"Thanks, Ma," Mom says. "I thought I might've gone overboard with the onions this time."

"Not at all," Grandma says. "It's wonderful." She pauses. "So, as you know, I let Tory and Charise go. But I spoke to

Bruce from the fish market, and he very generously offered to help with the unloading of boxes. Lucy, I know you can handle stocking the shelves." She looks at me through the bottoms of her wire-rimmed eyeglasses.

I'm not really a fan of manual labor, but I know complaining won't do any good. Plus, I figure we all have to do our part; the pharmacy's important to me too.

"And Jane," Grandma goes on. "I'm wondering if you can speed up your degree. One class a year is hardly a fast path to becoming a pharmacist."

When Grandma says that, I feel bad for my mom. It wasn't exactly her dream in life to be a pharmacist. I'm not really sure if she ever had a dream job. She just always wanted to be an activist, to work for causes she believed in.

My mom and dad got married right after college, and my mom had Claudia when she was twenty-two. My parents didn't really have any money, so they figured they'd move in with my grandparents for a little while so they could save up and eventually buy a house. Grandma tells me that Mom was always protesting, trying to make the world a better place, even with a new baby.

She'd constantly write letters to the editors of so many magazines and newspapers; she has them all in a shoe box in her bedroom. One snow day, I read them all.

Back then, my mom worked at the pharmacy; she handled the cash register and offered suggestions to customers. And my dad commuted to Yale (that's where my parents met) so he could finish getting his master's degree.

But all these years later, my mom is still living in the same room. My parents never ended up buying a house. My dad moved to London when I was three; he teaches there.

A few years ago, when the pharmacy really started to struggle, Mom decided to go back to school and become a pharmacist. But she's still in school because she ends up taking more electives than required classes.

It's easy to see why there's tension between Mom and Grandma. Plus, Mom's forty and she still lives with her mother. No other moms I know live with their mothers.

"Ma." Mom swallows a piece of chicken and turns to Grandma. "Relax. Everything will be fine." She smiles at Grandma, then at me. Mom's an eternal optimist, and when she gets depressed about something, she doesn't spend too long feeling bad about it. She just finds a way to try to change it. It's not her fault that her plans don't always work—there's a lot of injustice, and anyway she always says everyone can help if they try.

Grandma slumps back in her chair, wiping the corners of her mouth with a cloth napkin like she's a lady at a very fancy dinner party. "Darling, you know that locked cabinet you have in the office, behind your desk?" Grandma widens her eyes at my mother like she's inspecting something. "Well, I unlocked it. And I know how grave the situation is."

Mom chokes on her ginseng-enhanced iced tea. I can't believe this; my mom is an adult, a grown woman, and she still gets in trouble with her mother. How did this conversation change tone so quickly?

Grandma keeps talking. "I'm willing to wait this out for a little while. I have faith that we can pull out of this. But I'm considering selling the house. We can move into the upstairs apartment for a while, save money, and then we can figure out what we're going to do."

My eyes bulge at that, and I literally drop my fork. It clinks against my ceramic plate. "What?"

"Lucy, I'm beginning to think we don't really have a choice," Grandma says, talking to me like I'm an adult, like I can handle whatever she says.

And that's exactly when I realize that, yeah, I've been wishing and hoping that we'd find a way to save the pharmacy. But now I need to do more than just wish and hope. I need a real plan of action.

The only problem is, I'm a kid. And maybe in the movies kids can save the day. Like in *Home Alone*—which I've seen on DVD and TV a million times—Kevin just takes on those robbers, protects the house, and even goes out grocery shopping after his parents accidentally leave him home when they go on vacation. He becomes a hero, but that's a movie. In real life, there's not so much we can do.

And this situation is affecting me too personally. Not to sound selfish, but a few weeks ago Grandma told me I'd have to take a break from my art lessons. Up until then, I'd been going once a week since I was seven. When she told me, I didn't complain at all. Not a bit. Because I understood the situation.

I excuse myself from the table, put my dishes in the sink, and go up to my room. Maybe I need to do research, read a book or something. Would it be so impossible for someone to write *Saving Your Family's Business for Dummies*?

Beauty tip: If you're out of blush or
too young to wear it, pinch your cheeks a
few times to bring color to your face.

The best part about owning a pharmacy is
having all the products to play with. No doubt about it. The
cosmetics companies we order from send us samples of their
new products to get us all excited about ordering them when
the products are ready. That's how we found the Earth Beauty
line. They sent us this whole box of samples, and I loved them,
so Grandma stocks a bunch of their stuff now.

I always volunteer to be the official Old Mill Pharmacy
tester of these sample products. To be honest, it's not like I
have competition for the tester job. I'm the only one who
wants to do it.

Yesterday, a whole box of makeup samples came in. And
not old-lady makeup like sticky, smelly lipstick and blush
that looks like it's made for a clown. Young people's makeup,

and the best stuff too: shimmery silver eye shadow, summer-glow bronzer, and a million different shades of lip-glosses, just waiting in the brown box for me to try them.

As soon as I get to the pharmacy, I run and grab the box off the desk in the back office. Then I go into the bathroom, lock the door, and start testing.

The key is not to put on too much. You need to put on just enough to see how the product looks, but not so much that it overwhelms you.

The shimmery silver eye shadow is perfect. It's not so thick that if you accidentally rub your eye it all comes off in a clump on your finger. It's smooth and even on the eyelids, and it shimmers in just the right spots.

The bronzer's good too, but bronzer is bronzer, really. The most important thing to remember is not to use too much. Make it look natural. I'm brushing it on softly with the special bronzer brush we have, making sure to highlight my cheeks.

And finally, the best part: testing the lip-glosses. The ones that came yesterday are from the Extra Glossy line, and they're all candy names: Red Candy Cane, Beige Butterscotch, Burgundy Gumdrop, and lots more.

I put each one on lightly. They're the kind of lip-glosses that come in a skinny tube with a mini-brush to paint them on. I put on a little of each one, check it out in the mirror, and then wipe it off carefully with a tissue. It's hard to see the new color if there's a little bit of the one before peeking out from underneath.

The last color I try is my favorite: Pink Lollipop. It looks soft and colorful without being too much. And it smells delicious. Like a summer carnival.

People don't always realize this, but doing makeup is a real art form. It's just as hard to master and just as satisfying as making art when you do it well. The face is your canvas, and that's why I figure taking art lessons is important—it can only make my makeup skills stronger.

There's a knock on the bathroom door. "Go put together a package for Claudia," Grandma says.

"Um, Grams, Claudia's birthday is today, so it's obviously not going to get to Chicago on time," I say, talking back through the closed door, still admiring the Pink Lollipop lipgloss in the mirror. She doesn't respond. "And besides, why are we going to send stuff to Claudia for free when it's actual stuff that we, like, need to sell?"

I meant to say that politely, but even I think I sounded rude. I'm just annoyed that Claudia's not here. I know she had to go to college and everything, but Claudia's the person who taught me to do makeup and who got me into it. I've been practicing on her since I was seven. We started doing it mostly because we were bored, and then it became my favorite thing to do.

"Lucy, please, just do it. We ordered her birthday gift online. This is just some extra stuff," Grandma says as soon as I leave the bathroom. I slump down the pharmacy aisles, taking random stuff for Claudia and throwing it into a box: hair mousse, wintergreen toothpaste, a beaded hair band, and three bags of Tootsie Pops.

There, that wasn't so hard.

And I know Claudia will appreciate the hair mousse. She goes through that stuff like it's water. Her hair is pretty much the opposite of mine, except for the color. We both have brown hair, but hers is tight, spirally curly, like Mom's. And when I look in the mirror and see my boring, brown, straight-as-a-ruler hair, I sort of wish I had hair like Claudia's. But there's nothing I can do about it. Grandma says people always want what they can't have. I think she's right, especially when it comes to hair.

My best friend, Sunny, was supposed to come with me to the pharmacy today, but at the last minute she couldn't. She forgot she had to go to her cousin Asha's dance recital. Asha doesn't do just any kind of dance, like ballet or tap—she does Indian dance. She's really good at it, graceful and calm. She looks like a goddess when she dances.

Sunny does Indian dancing too, but she's not as into it

as Asha is. I think Sunny just gets nervous, plus Asha's three years older than we are. And Asha takes that age difference really seriously. She *acts* like she's so much older, like we're really immature. And she calls Sunny by her real name—Sunita. Nobody calls her that, except her parents, sometimes.

"Lucy, oh, *Lucy*," Grandma sings from across the pharmacy. She's standing next to the counter with Meredith Ganzi. "I'm summoning you."

Meredith Ganzi is from Waterside, and she's probably the pharmacy's best customer, even though she's only nine years old and doesn't have any of her own money to buy things. Her mom works at the movie theater next door, so Meredith usually just hangs around either at the theater or at the pharmacy on the weekends and some days after school. She's really annoying, but every time I tell Grandma that, she gives me a look. "Meredith isn't as fortunate as you are, Lucy," she tells me. "Be nice."

I don't say what I'm thinking. I don't say to Grandma, "I don't think I'm really so fortunate." If I did, she'd kill me. I walk over to them, carrying the brown box filled with stuff for Claudia. "Hi, Meredith," I say.

"You look really nice today, Lucy," Meredith says, looking at my grandmother for agreement. Meredith is one of those girls who think giving people compliments is the only way to get them to like her. I wish she knew that wasn't true.

Besides, I don't really look that nice today. I'm wearing a boring pink pocket T and jeans from two years ago, and they have a tiny hole in the middle of the thigh. And I'm not one of those girls who are into ripped jeans.

"Yes, she does." Grandma smiles like she believes it, but also like she needs me to get back to work. "Your job today is to reorganize the hair-product aisle. Everything is out of place. Gel is with dandruff shampoo. It's a disaster."

"Okay, Grams, I'm on it," I say. When I take a quick glance to the back of the store, I notice that Mom's still on the computer in the back office. She's been writing a letter to the editor of the *Old Mill Observer* all morning. She's furious that they are planning to get rid of the dog park to make a parking lot. We don't even have a dog, but she's still really angry that such a thing would happen.

As I'm reorganizing the hair section, I overhear Grandma doing what she's almost always doing: giving advice.

"But how can I prove to her that I'm old enough?" Meredith whines. They've been having this same conversation for a week now.

"Merry, listen, I'm telling you. The best way to prove to your mom that you're old enough to get your ears pierced is to show some responsibility," I hear Grandma say, and when I look up, she has her finger up in the air, waving it for emphasis.

"Okay, so what can you do? Well, set the table. Walk the dog. Make sure your room is clean."

Meredith sighs. "My mom's not as nice as you are, though."

"Nonsense." Grandma shakes her head. "Tell your mom to come to the store after her shift. I have her prescriptions ready, and the moisturizer I special-ordered for her."

At two thirty, I feel my cell phone vibrating in my pocket.

I flip it open and Claudia groans, "Thanks for the billion texts, Lucy," before I even get to say hello. "Mom's gonna be thrilled when she sees that bill. And you know we're an hour behind you, right?"

"Yeah, I know. I wanted to make you feel loved on your birthday, being so far away from home," I say. "Sorry if love costs money." She laughs. "Where have you been? It's Saturday. I know you don't have class on Saturday."

"Actually, you know how Amanda and I have the same birthday?" she asks. I'd forgotten that, but I pretend to remember. I wonder if everyone at Northwestern is paired with a roommate who has the same birthday.

"Well, her mom flew in from Atlanta, and she took us to a spa this morning! How amazing is that?"

"Amazing," I grumble. It's hard not to be jealous of

Claudia. She's living this awesome life in Chicago, going to spas and everything, while I worry back in Connecticut.

I can hear her slurping her drink over the phone. "Get this: It was an eco-spa!"

"An eco-spa?" I ask.

"Yeah, all the products were earth-friendly. They used special machines for some of the treatments so they didn't waste energy. They used special lighting, had recycled paper to cover the tables. And a billion other things."

"That sounds cool, I guess." Hearing Claudia so excited about this eco-spa makes me depressed. I feel like I don't have anything to be that excited about.

"I know," she says. "Anyway, thanks for all the birthday wishes. I gotta go. These guys down the hall are throwing a party for us, and they want us to check out the decorations."

I roll my eyes, which thankfully Claudia can't see through the phone. I hate when she rushes me off the phone, but I guess she has an excuse today, since it's her birthday. "Have fun," I say.

College sounds like the best place in the world. Too bad I have six years until I can get there.

Beauty tip: When it comes to
hair, sometimes simpler is better.

At four thirty, I'm still organizing the hair-
products aisle. My day has been the complete opposite
of Claudia's, but I guess she deserves some fun on her
birthday.

I'm arranging the hair gels by color (a new change I'm
implementing in the pharmacy, though Mom and Grandma
don't know it yet) when I start to hear screaming coming from
the parking lot. And it's getting louder.

"Mom! I'm not going to say it again. That woman ruined
my hair! I don't care about a refund. Homecoming is tonight.
Tonight! Do you even know what that means?"

The screaming is really loud now, since the girl is in the
store. I wonder what could have possibly happened to her hair.

I stand up on my tiptoes so I can peek over the top shelf
in the hair section and see who is making such a commotion.

And in a million, billion years I never could have guessed who was inside Old Mill Pharmacy right this very minute. Never in a million, billion, trillion years.

Courtney Adner.

Homecoming queen at Old Mill High School for two years in a row.

"Mom, seriously, I'm hanging up on you. You sent me to your stupid salon when I could have gone with Brooke and Taylor, and now look." Courtney pauses, holding the phone a few feet away from her face and rolling her eyes at it. I scrunch down a little to make sure she can't see me. "Hanging up, Mom. Hanging up." She slams her flip phone closed with way too much force for a cell phone to handle, and then she walks over to the hair-product aisle, right where I am.

I'm not really sure what to do, since Courtney's wearing a baseball cap, and I can't see her hair. If I knew what the problem was, maybe I could make a suggestion.

Courtney starts going through the hair-product shelves bottle by bottle, tube by tube, carefully reading the descriptions on each one. To my surprise, she seems kind of calm now, and I begin to think everything's going to be okay.

But that only lasts for a second. Soon Courtney starts dialing numbers furiously, one after another. When her friends' voice mails pick up, she says, *"E-mer-gen-cy,"* and then hangs up. None of her friends answer, and she gets angrier and angrier, stamping her black boots on the linoleum floor and making those weird black marks that look terrible but actually come off with just a rub of your sock.

I'll have to text Claudia later and tell her about this.

I'm just going about my business, still color-coding the shelves, when Courtney starts weeping right in front of me. I didn't think a girl like Courtney Adner wept like this, all pathetic and splotchy. She's wiping her eyes with the sleeve of her maroon cardigan. I don't know what to do. Next, she falls to the floor, holding her head in her hands and rocking back and forth.

That's when Grandma comes over.

"Doll, what's the trouble here?" Grandma asks.

Courtney looks up at Grandma, and for some reason that makes her cry even more.

"If you tell me the problem, maybe I'll be able to find a way to fix it," Grandma says.

"No offense, but you can't fix it." She sniffs. "Unless you can cut off all my hair and then make it grow back by tonight." She looks down at the floor and doesn't wait for an answer. "See what I mean? Can't fix it."

"Okay, take off the hat," Grandma insists. "Take it off so I can see what they've done to you."

"Seriously. I just told you. You can't fix this." Then she mumbles, "And don't tell me what to do."

"Take off the hat," Grandma says again, firmly. "I'll be the judge of this situation."

Courtney finally listens to Grandma. Even Courtney Adner listens to my grandma.

Under Courtney's baseball cap is a mop of frizzed-out, thick, tangled strawberry-blonde hair. Well, the top is strawberry blonde; the bottom is green. "If you can fix this, then you're a miracle worker," Courtney says.

Grandma stands back a few feet, her hands over her mouth, nodding like she's assessing the situation. I look around, wondering where Mom is, and I see her sitting in the office, on the phone. She's in her own world right now; she probably doesn't even realize this Courtney Adner hair trauma is even happening.

"Okay, doll, here's the thing," Grandma says softly, touching Courtney's shoulder. "You're not going to be able to wear your hair down for this event. But—"

Grandma stops talking and walks over to the hair-accessory aisle. Courtney and I just stand there staring at each other. Claudia was right about one thing—Courtney Adner really is pretty. All of her features just go together: the perfect nose; big, green eyes; lips that aren't too big and aren't too small. Courtney Adner's too pretty for her hair to look like this.

When Grandma comes back, she has a handful of hair accessories. Some I know Courtney will definitely not want to wear. They're made of pearls and satin ribbons, and I'm kind of embarrassed that Grandma even brought them over. But some of the others are okay. Maybe.

"Um, I don't think so," Courtney says, a little rudely.

"You don't think so?" Grandma asks. "You didn't even look."

Courtney looks through the pile, but I can tell she's not happy. Grandma leaves to help some women looking at the aromatherapy candles at the front of the store.

While Grandma and Courtney were talking, though, I thought of a solution—I think. Maybe it won't help the problem permanently. But it'll help the problem for today, and that's something. But I don't know if I should even bother. It's not like Courtney Adner, homecoming queen for two years running, is really going to listen to a seventh grader.

"Maybe I can just wear a hat?" Courtney asks, not talking to anyone in particular. "Maybe it'll be a new trend or something." She takes her phone out of her pocket and starts dialing. Again, no one picks up, but she gets a few voice mails and says, "We're wearing hats tonight," to each one.

Her cell phone rings a second later. I don't think the person on the other end even utters two words before Courtney starts screaming: "I said we're wearing hats. Don't argue with me, Petra." Courtney starts stamping her feet again. "Petra, it will not look stupid."

After Courtney hangs up, she looks through the pile of hair accessories again, whimpering. "Ugh, these are all so ugly!" she says under her breath. When I look up, she says, "Oh, sorry. I didn't mean to insult your products."

Now's the time. I have to say something.

"Um, Courtney," I say. My mouth feels dry, since it's the first thing I've said in a while. "I have two products that will help. One to fix the frizz, and the other to fix the green color issue."

"Luce, let's not start mixing more products," Grandma says. I have no idea how she overheard me from the front of the store. But now she's walking over to us. "You don't know what the combination will do."

"Trust me, Grams. These products are meant to fix mishaps." I go over to the shelves to find the purple bottle of Fix-a-Frizz and the green tube (how appropriate) of Natural Color.

See, I've had a lot of time to read the descriptions on all of these products over the past few years. I know what they all do and how they work. I've even watched the infomercials, just to get some extra information.

"Put the Fix-a-Frizz on first, let it sit for twenty minutes, and then brush it through your hair. You don't need to wash it out," I tell Courtney. "And then you only put the Natural Color on the sections that have color damage. Make sure you don't put it on your whole head."

I hand Courtney the bottles and she stares at me. "These will really work?"

I nod. "Yeah, they'll fix your hair for tonight. Then use this." I hand her the bottle of the Earth Beauty rinse. "It's meant to naturally restore your hair to its original state."

Courtney still doesn't seem convinced. "And what'll I do if my hair looks even worse after I use this stuff? Then what?"

"Then you'll wear a hat." I shrug and guide her over to the cash register, where Mom's putting all of Mr. Becker's diaper-rash products for his newborn son into a bag. At least Mom's finally out of the office. When she's done, Mom takes Courtney's products, and Courtney hands her a credit card.

"Well, if this doesn't work, then I want my money back," Courtney says to Mom, not even looking at me.

"Actually, the Fix-a-Frizz can be used right here," I add. I really want her to believe me. I feel a little like my mother right now, fighting for a good cause. "You don't even need water."

"Yeah, so?" she grumbles.

"Let me show you. Sit down, and I'll put it in your hair," I say. "Then you'll feel a little better. I promise." I have no idea where this surge of confidence is coming from, but I've tried the Fix-a-Frizz on Claudia's hair a billion times. I know it works.

"Whatever—it can't get any worse," Courtney mutters. She sits down on the chair next to the prescription counter and hands me the bottle. I pour a few drops out into my palm and then rub my hands together. Then I very gently comb it through her hair with my fingers.

After I brush it through, I hand her a mirror. "It's not perfect." I shrug. "But it's a start. If you go home and use the Natural Color and the Earth Beauty rinse, you'll be fine. You don't need to wash your hair with shampoo if you use the rinse."

"I can't believe this," Courtney says, admiring herself in the mirror. "I actually have almost normal-looking hair again." She turns around and looks at me in disbelief. "Thank you. What's your name again?"

"It's Lucy." I smile.

I'm not surprised that the Fix-a-Frizz worked, but I am a little surprised that Courtney Adner trusted me and believed me and let me use it on her hair, right here. Maybe I'm more like my mom than I realize. Maybe I have that same passion for making bad situations a little better and fixing injustices. It was only a hair trauma situation, but for Courtney it seemed like the end of the world. And I helped her.

"Thank you so much," Courtney says, handing me the mirror.

"Have fun tonight! I'm sure you're going to look great."

Courtney Adner would look great anyway. Even with that hair.

Beauty tip: Lip-gloss is the perfect finishing touch to any clothing ensemble.

Sunny and I usually take the bus to school, but Mrs. Ramal's driving us today. She has to drive Yamir anyway, because he's bringing in a huge sculpture of the earth showing the effects of global warming, and there's no way he could take that on the bus. It's probably some extra-credit thing for Science. Yamir always does everything extra that he possibly can. He's one of those kids who make everyone else look bad.

Mom and Grandma are already at the pharmacy, and it feels weird to think that I could just stay home today, play hooky, and they'd never know. By the time they usually get home, around six, I'll be home from school anyway. Or I could just go over to the pharmacy around three thirty, when I'd normally be out of school. Either way, I could spend the whole day on the couch watching daytime television shows that I only get to see when I'm sick. I could order in pizza or Chinese food. I could do anything, really.

Knowing this kind of makes me feel powerful, and knowing I'd never do it makes me feel like a wimp. But since they're not here, I decide I can wear a little more makeup than I'd normally wear to school. Usually, I wear colorless lip-gloss and a little blush. But today I put on green glitter eye shadow and my favorite new product: my Pink Lollipop Extra Glossy lip-gloss. Just these little touches make me feel more dressed up.

Mrs. Ramal honks to let me know they're here. I lock the front door and sling my heavy backpack over one shoulder. Walking over to the car, I see that Sunny's in the front seat and Yamir's in the back, with the huge model of the earth next to him.

He pushes the model over to the other seat and hops out of the car. "You're smaller than the earth, so you get to sit in the middle," he says.

So I slide in, and I'm smooshed between the earth and Yamir. I have to fiddle around for my seat belt, and Yamir doesn't even try to help me find it. I'm touching his thigh, and I don't want to be. God. Why do car companies make the middle seat belt so impossible to find? Sitting in the middle is bad enough, yet they found a way to make it even worse.

"Ooh, Lu-Lu, we're so close right now." Yamir laughs. He's right—we are close. I can smell onion bagel on his breath, and I try as hard as I can not to gag.

"*Mah-ahm!*" Sunny yells. "Tell Yamir to stop being disgusting."

"Yamir," Mrs. Ramal warns. "Please behave like a gentleman."

Sunny says, "Yamir, only you would make this huge, annoying project for a stupid club." She looks back at us. "Lucy, it's not even for Science. It's for Earth Club."

"Really?" I turn to look at Yamir.

"It will also be entered in the county science fair, which I only get to enter because of Earth Club. There's a five-thousand-dollar prize if I win," Yamir tells us. "And that's not all. There's a trip to—"

Mrs. Ramal interrupts him and says, "Sunita, it wouldn't be such a bad thing if you joined some after-school club. I'd like to see you take an interest in something meaningful."

Sunny turns to look back at me again, and she bursts out laughing.

"It's not funny," Mrs. Ramal says. "I have been thinking

this for a while, and now is the time I've chosen to say something. I would like you to join some activity."

Now both Sunny and I are laughing, but I'm not even sure why.

"Lucy, you could do it too," Mrs. Ramal adds. "If your mother says it's okay."

Until recently, I took art lessons. That was my extracurricular. And Sunny does Indian dance. But I guess Mrs. Ramal thinks we should do a school thing.

"Yeah," Yamir says, sticking his tongue out at the back of Sunny's seat. Then he smiles all good-boy-like at me.

Yamir Ramal really knows how to start the day off wrong.

On our way into school I tap Sunny on the shoulder, right in front of the Juicy Juice machine. "Sun, I have to tell you something," I mutter.

Her shoulders perk up. "What? And are you wearing perfume today?"

"No, it's my Pink Lollipop lip-gloss. Doesn't it smell delicious?"

Sunny nods.

I let out a long breath. "Okay, I have to make this quick—first period starts soon. I think the pharmacy might be going out of business." It hurts to say that out loud. I love Old Mill

Pharmacy. I love the memories I have from all the time I've spent in the store—like when I was little and Grandpa used to push me around in the shopping carts after the store closed. And when Grandma would make Claudia and me root beer floats at the counter, even though Mom really didn't want us to have soda.

Sunny's response is slow, almost like a delayed chemical reaction. First her eyes bulge and her mouth opens, but no words come out. And then she gives me a look. "Really?" She looks around and then whispers, "Why?"

"Business isn't good anymore. People just go to, like, big stores where they can buy groceries and clothes and their prescriptions all at the same time."

"But those stores don't usually give the personal touch," Sunny insists. "And my dad says a lot of those stores are bad to their workers."

I shrug. I know she's trying to make me feel better, but I don't know what else to say. Sunny and I walk through the hall silently. After a few minutes she asks, "How can you be so calm about this?"

"I'm not calm. I'm just tired, so it seems like I'm calm," I tell her. It's a relief to tell Sunny this, but it does make me tired talking about it.

"Well, I'm going to tell my mom to shop at the pharmacy

every single day from now on. She already gets prescriptions there, but I'm gonna tell her that she has to buy at least one thing there a day. Even if it's just gum."

"Thanks, Sunny," I say. "Oh, but guess what? I do have some cool news!"

"What?" Sunny's shoulders perk up again.

"So this girl Courtney Adner," I start. "She's in high school, you probably don't know her. I only know her because of Claudia. But anyway, she came into the pharmacy after she had this really bad hair situation at a salon on the night of homecoming, and—"

"Lucy! Get to the point!" Sunny says.

"And I fixed her hair. Right there in the pharmacy! I knew these two products would work, and they did!"

"You gave her a makeover?"

I throw my hands up. "Yeah! I guess so!"

"That's awesome, Luce," Sunny says, putting her arm around me.

It's good to hear that from Sunny, because I do feel really awesome about how I was able to help Courtney.

We get to our lockers, and I'm taking some books off my top shelf when someone bumps into me, really hard. "Move out of the way," I hear Erica Crane say. "You're blocking my locker."

Very unluckily for me, Erica Crane's locker is next to mine this year. Erica's been mean to me for as long as I've known her, since we were five, but there's never been a real reason for it. She's just always hated me. She never shared the toys in kindergarten, and she threw my lunch in the garbage for four days in a row in third grade. And in fifth grade, when her mom forced her to invite the whole class to her birthday party, she handed out the invitations in school but "accidentally" lost mine and never found it.

It's just a fact of life: Erica Crane hates me. Always has, always will.

"I'm not in your way," I say. "I'm in front of *my* locker."

"Shut up, Lucy," Erica says. "And by the way, lay off the scallion cream cheese. Your breath stinks, and you have scallion pieces in your teeth."

I turn away from her and clamp my lips shut. I grab Sunny by the arm and lead her into the bathroom so I can check my teeth.

6

Beauty tip: Using too much conditioner
can make hair oily and greasy.

Sunny calls me after school. "My mom's forcing me to join Earth Club," she says as soon as I answer. "I don't have a choice. It's either that or extra classes at the Hindu temple."

"Really? Why?"

"She thinks I spend too much time watching TV."

"Well, you do watch a lot of TV," I say, propping my feet up on my desk.

"Thanks. Will you go with me?" Sunny asks.

I pop a few more mini chocolate-chip cookies into my mouth. "Sunny!" I whine. "Do you understand what my life is like these days? I spend every waking minute that I'm not in school at the pharmacy."

Sunny groans. "Lucy, please. You're home right now, just eating cookies."

She's right. Sunny knows me too well. "I really don't have time," I say. "My grandma even said that I'm going to be stocking the shelves. Seriously, I'm like an actual Old Mill Pharmacy employee now." Even though I complain, I don't really hate it. I'd be proud to be an official Old Mill Pharmacy employee.

"Please, Lucy, please," Sunny begs. "I hate doing stuff alone. You know I'd do it for you."

She's right about that. She would do it for me. I guess it's not such a big deal. The pharmacy can survive without me one afternoon a week. And all the clubs give snacks, so that's one incentive.

"Fine," I say. "I'll do it. But only for you. And you definitely owe me!"

"Thank you! Thank you! Thank you! Thank you!" Sunny shouts.

All through school the next day, I'm dreading Earth Club. I'm tired and I have tons of homework to do, and even the cookies they're going to have aren't enough to make me want to go. Still, I said I would. And Grandma didn't seem mad about it at all; she said there wasn't much work to do today anyway.

Mrs. Deleccio is the faculty member in charge of Earth

Club. She was my and Sunny's science teacher last year, in sixth grade, and she's really nice.

"We have a few new members today," she says. "Welcome, Sunny and Lucy. We're going to finish up the recycling project this afternoon. There are still about ten classrooms that need recycling boxes, so I need people to volunteer for that, and also to volunteer to collect the recyclables from the other classrooms."

We break into groups according to which project we want to do. Honestly, I don't want to do either. I'm tired after a whole day at school, and both jobs sound really boring. Sunny wants to do the emptying of the recycling boxes, so I figure I might as well do it with her. And there are about ten people in that group, which means less work for me. But Yamir's in that group too, and I have no idea why Sunny would want to be in the same group as her brother.

"Luce-Juice, go get the recycling box from Mr. Bodesti's classroom, and empty it into this bag," Yamir tells me, like he's in charge. "Now!"

"Please, Yamir. Stop yelling," I say. I have zero patience for him.

"If you don't want to be in this club, then why are you here?" he asks me.

"Who said I didn't want to be in this club?"

He rolls his eyes at me. "You're weird," he says.

"This is the most annoying part," Evan Mass says. "But once it's done, it's done."

I shrug. I'll be happy when it's done; he's right about that.

"How come you guys decided to join?" Evan asks Sunny and me. Evan's been in our grade since kindergarten. He used to be a normal boy—no big deal. But this year for some reason a lot of girls like him. I mean, he's nice and everything. But he wears sweatpants to school every day, the kind with tight elastic around the ankle.

"My mom made my sister do it," Yamir says, answering for us.

"Shut up, Yamir," Sunny says. "She didn't make me."

"Yes, she did," Yamir says, looking at Evan. "My sister would prefer to sit on the couch eating Pringles every day."

"Shut up, Yamir," I say.

I hate when he insults Sunny like this, in front of other people. It's terrible that they're so close in age. I'm glad there are six years between Claudia and me, instead of just one.

Evan says, "Sunny, remember in second grade when you, me, and that girl Denise had to do that pinecone art project together?"

Sunny raises her shoulders and squints like she just tasted something sour. "Yeah, I think so."

"So, you were into this kind of stuff then," Evan says.

Sunny just stares at him and doesn't say anything.

Suddenly there's all this awkwardness in the air, and I really want it to go away.

"All right. We gotta finish, guys," I say.

As soon I say that, Sunny empties the recycling boxes into the garbage bags that I'm holding. One is for glass stuff and one is for plastic stuff. We do three more classrooms on the east wing of the school, and then, finally, we're finished.

This experience has been painful. Painful, annoying, and boring, kind of like the pharmacy can be sometimes.

I'm only doing this for Sunny.

7

Business tip: When customers come in, ask them to fill
out a slip with their name, address, and birthday. Then
when the time comes, mail them a birthday coupon.

Tonight's Sunny's birthday party. She pretty
much has the same party every single year—a sleepover at her
house. Me, Megan, and Cassandra are going. And Mallory
too. The new girl.

I guess she's really not that new anymore, but I still think
of her as the new girl. Not in a mean way. But when Grandma
asks me about my friends and I mention Mallory, she always
asks, "Oh, the new girl?" So that's why I call her that.

Sunny's the youngest girl in our grade. She's just turning twelve, and some kids have been thirteen for months
already.

It always feels like Sunny's birthday sneaks up on me.
When her birthday rolls around, I wonder how it got to be
the end of October already. Wasn't it just the first day of

school? That's always what I'm thinking, every single year. I'm thinking that now too, as I'm wrapping her present.

I'm doing an extra-good job on the wrapping part. I love wrapping presents. My favorite thing is to take the edge of the scissors and press it against the ribbon to curl it. I especially love the sound it makes. And when the ribbon curls up perfectly, I feel like a real artist.

Every time I curl the ribbon like that, I always think of my mom. Her hair is so spirally curly that it kind of looks like it was curled with the edge of the scissors. I wish my hair looked like that. People like Mom and Claudia and everyone else who has spiral curls are so lucky.

The wrapping is complete with curlicue bows and ribbons and all the trimmings. I never wrap presents at home since the pharmacy has a huge selection of wrapping paper. And even though I'm doing a top-notch wrapping job, I bet Sunny will be way more excited about what's inside.

I got Sunny exactly what she wanted, what she's been talking about since last April: dangly, beaded earrings. Claudia has a pair, and they're from Italy. Claudia got them from her annoying best friend who travels all over the world and gets whatever she wants.

When Sunny saw Claudia wearing the earrings, she freaked. Really freaked. She begged Claudia to let her try them on. Claudia said yes, of course. She'd never be rude to Sunny the way she sometimes is to me. After that, Sunny talked about them constantly. And even though I don't see the big deal, I decided to get them for her for her birthday. Claudia told me I could order them online, and even though they're pretty expensive, Mom and Grandma said Sunny was worth it. I ordered them before all the going-out-of-business money talk started. I bet Grandma and Mom regret letting me buy them now.

But one thing is for sure—my present will definitely be Sunny's favorite.

"Look at that wrapping job!" Grandma says, walking into the pharmacy office. "You're hired for holiday time. You're practically a professional gift wrapper!"

It's good to know she thinks the pharmacy will still be open come holiday time.

I'm waiting for Mom to drive me over to Sunny's when I hear someone say, "Is that the girl?"

I'm the only girl in the store right now, so they must be talking about me.

I don't know if I should let on that I heard them, or if I should just go about my business until they come over to talk to me.

La-di-da. I sit there in one of the flimsy prescription-area plastic chairs, holding Sunny's gift, pretending I didn't hear anything. Then I see shadows standing over me. When I look up, I see Courtney Adner with a few of her friends.

"This is my hero," Courtney says to the other girls. "She's the one I've been talking about."

"Hi," I say to them, smiling.

"Lucy, those products were amazing! Especially that Natural Color solution. It was like magic," she says. "Seriously."

"It really is great stuff," I tell her. I'm so happy the products worked. I knew the Fix-a-Frizz was a success, but that couldn't do the job by itself. And I'm even happier that she just called me her hero.

"How old are you?" one of the girls asks me. "You saved my friend from horrible hair humiliation at homecoming. You're like a hair-care prodigy."

"I'm twelve."

"She's Claudia Desberg's sister," Courtney says.

"Ahhhh, now it makes sense."

I chat with Courtney and her friends for a few more minutes, and I have to admit it's kind of nice to have these high school girls oohing and aahing over me. Who doesn't like that? And I feel so happy knowing that my hair advice really helped her. She went to homecoming and looked amazing, and that was partly because of me!

Is it bad that I sort of hope more people will come in with hair emergencies so I can help them too?

After we're done talking, Courtney and her friends raid the makeup aisle and then the hair-product aisle, and I realize that this is one of the best days the pharmacy has had in a long while, thanks to Courtney Adner and her hair disaster.

8

I've always been . . . interested in making women look as beautiful as possible while making them look like themselves. —*Laura Mercier*

It's no coincidence that I'm the first one to get to Sunny's house. I like to be the first one there, to get settled before the others arrive. I don't feel like any old guest at Sunny's parties. I'm a VIP.

Sunny's mom opens the door, and she's wearing her red KISS THE COOK apron over her clothes. Sunny's house always smells like a combination of curry and coconut. "I've been baking nonstop for you girls," she says as I walk inside. "Sunny asked for cupcakes and a birthday cake, plus I had to make my oatmeal-chocolate-chip cookies just for you." She winks at me.

"Thanks, Mrs. Ramal," I say, smiling. She knows those are my favorite.

"Sunny's up in her room," she tells me. I'm still holding Sunny's wrapped present, and I'm not sure if I should leave it down here or bring it up and let her open it before everyone else arrives. Maybe I should give it to her right away—she's going to love it so much, and I don't want the others to feel bad that their gifts aren't as good as mine.

I run up the stairs, trying not to step on the pretty pink rose design that's on the carpet. I always try to step on the cream background instead.

"Sunny," I sing, gently knocking on her door as I walk in.

"Lucy! You scared me," she says, sitting up in her purple beanbag chair. She's dressed for the party in her pale pink velour sweat suit. She likes wearing things that are comfy but still cute.

"Why? You knew I'd be early." I put my jacket and the present on her bed and my overnight bag under her desk. "So should I give you your present now or later?"

"Ummm, later," she says. "I have to talk to you."

I sit down next to her on the beanbag chair, nudging her so she'll move over and make more room for me. She smells like Dove soap, and her hair isn't totally dry yet. Sunny has extremely thick hair. She usually starts with a hair dryer but gets bored halfway through and lets the rest air-dry.

"Did you use that conditioner again?" I ask Sunny. Even though her hair's still wet, the top already looks greasy.

"No," she says defensively.

I shake my head at her. "Next time I'm at the pharmacy, I'm getting you oily-hair shampoo. It's perfect for thick, awesome hair like yours." I don't want to criticize Sunny, because no matter what, she always looks pretty. She has huge green eyes and near-perfect skin. Even so, she rarely feels good about the way she looks. And I want to help.

"Whatever," Sunny mumbles.

"Can I do your makeup for your party?" I ask. "Nothing too much, I promise."

Sunny groans. "Lucy," she whines. "I don't want to wear makeup. Can you get that through your head already?"

"But come on, just for the party. Just some of that Pink Lollipop lip-gloss I was telling you about. You loved it when I wore it the other day. Remember? And pale eye shadow." I smile at her sweetly as I unload my pockets. It's her party. Shouldn't she look and feel her best? "I took some stuff for you from the pharmacy."

"You thief!" Sunny says, inspecting the stuff I brought her. "That eye shadow—the Earth Beauty stuff? I thought you said no one buys that."

I shrug. "Yeah, that's why it was okay for me to take it. But trust me, it still works."

"Um, no thanks." Sunny mooshes up her face like she doesn't want to hurt my feelings. "Maybe some other time."

"Okay, but just dab some of this moisturizer on your cheeks." I smile at her. "Your skin is a little dry."

She rolls her eyes at me. "Fine, I'll do it in a second."

She taps me on the knee and looks me right in the eye. "Remember this summer when we discussed crushes? And we thought we were weird because we didn't have any?"

"Yeah," I say, waiting for her to tell me more.

Her eyes are wide, like she's excited but trying to stay calm. "Okay—Evan Mass." She smiles and shakes her hands in the air; her calmness is definitely fading.

"Really?" I kick off my sneakers and turn to face her.

"Ever since Earth Club," she goes on. "Now I like him. I really, really like him. It just happened, like, out of nowhere."

I smile, suddenly realizing that it's kind of exciting that Sunny has a crush. At least it's something to take my mind off the pharmacy. I tilt my head to the side and try to get a good look at her.

She folds her arms across her chest and presses her lips together like she's thinking really hard about something. "But it's not like anything's ever going to really happen between Evan and me. I mean—this is *me* we're talking about."

"Sunny, that is so not true," I tell her. "Confidence goes a long way, you know. That's what Claudia says. I know—open your present!"

Sunny hops up from the beanbag chair and goes to inspect my gift. "I said you should give it to me later," she complains. "Why are you tempting me?"

"I can't wait." I make a pouty face. "Please. Pretty, pretty please with caramel sauce on top."

Sunny sighs and eventually agrees. She's very impressed with my wrapping job, so she's careful. She doesn't just tear into the gift, making a mess of the silver wrapping paper and ruining the bows. In fact, she takes all of the bows and ribbons off and puts them on her desk.

"Oh my God," she says, not looking at me. She's holding the earrings up in front of her and inspecting them. "Lucy! I can't even believe you."

Giving a gift is sometimes even better than getting one. "You like them?" I ask, even though I obviously know the answer.

"I *love* them!" she says, in a classic Sunny shriek. "I can't believe you remembered. Did you, like, go to Italy and not tell me?"

I give her a look. "Hello. The Internet?"

"Oh yeah." She giggles and puts the earrings on, admiring herself in the mirror. Then she sits back down next to me. "So what should I do about Evan? Is there, like, something I can do about a crush, or do I just have to live with it?"

It's not like I expect her to keep flipping out over the earrings, thanking me over and over again, but our conversation about the gift ends a little sooner than I thought it would.

"We'll figure something out," I tell her. "Maybe we can go to the bookstore and read up on it. Or do some online research."

"See! It's so hard. It feels like another subject in school." Sunny moves her feet around on the carpet like she's tap-dancing. "Like something extra to worry about and focus on."

"Well, it's not like you're gonna have a test on it," I say, laughing.

She doesn't think it's as funny as I do. Her shoulders slump, and she says, "C'mon, let's go wait downstairs for everybody else."

Beauty tip: Make sure to wash your face every night before bed, even if it's really late and you don't feel like it.

After pizza and cupcakes and then Sunny's chocolate-chip birthday cake, we're all in pajamas in Sunny's upstairs playroom. Sunny's house is three floors, and the bottom one is totally under construction. Sunny's mom has been working on it for months, and I like seeing the progress.

Right now it's being painted. One room is going to have all red walls, and another is going to have pale yellow. And Sunny's mom is getting this really big, comfy couch that will wrap all the way around the red room.

They already have a big-screen TV, but they're getting a flat-screen, one that hangs from the ceiling. And Yamir begged for a karaoke machine, so they're getting that too. Sometimes I'll get little pangs of jealousy when I think about all the stuff Sunny has. But then the feeling kind of fades away because

Sunny never brags about it; she doesn't even talk about it that much. Truthfully, I bring it up more than she does.

This is the first time Mallory's been to Sunny's house, so she's looking at everything really closely. She's fascinated with all of the little statues of the Hindu gods and the Indian paintings on the walls, and she keeps commenting on them. I think they're cool, but I've seen them so many times that I don't even notice them anymore.

Sunny hasn't brought up Evan again, but it's probably because her parents have been around the whole time. I'm just waiting for her to mention it again. I know this isn't just a Sunny and Lucy discussion. She wasn't satisfied with our talk before, which is good because I need the other girls to help me pump her up in the confidence department.

We watch the DVD of our fifth-grade play, *You're a Good Man, Charlie Brown*, because Sunny loves watching old home movies. She pauses it fifty million times so we can see ourselves close-up. At first she only pauses it when we're on, so we can see ourselves, but then she pauses it on a solo, one of Charlie Brown's solos. I'd completely forgotten, but now I remember.

Evan Mass played Charlie Brown.

"Okay, I have an announcement to make," Sunny says. "I think I'm in love with Charlie Brown."

We all laugh, even me. But I obviously know what's coming.

"The play, or the comic?" Cassandra asks. She's never exactly been the sharpest tool in the shed. I hate to say it, but it's true.

Megan hits her. "Cass, come on." Megan looks over at Sunny and then back at Cassandra.

"Ohhhhh," Cassandra says, dragging out the word for way too long.

"Wait." Mallory looks around at each of us. "Is that Evan Mass?"

"Yup," Megan says. "He's in all the plays, and he always gets the lead. I think he takes voice lessons."

"I had to tell you guys." Sunny's staring at the TV, smiling. She gets up from the couch and moves closer to it. She's making smooching sounds, and then she literally walks up to the TV and kisses it.

Everyone laughs hysterically. No one would have expected that, especially from Sunny.

"Well, you're lucky that we have different people in all of our classes in seventh grade. It was so stupid that sixth graders had, like, almost all the same people in every class," Megan says. "This way you can, like, ask him for help with your homework, or something."

"That is such a good idea!" Sunny finally unpauses the DVD. "Megan, you're a genius."

We start watching the rest of the play, but then Sunny pauses it again, not stopping at anything specific. "Will I be able to do that, though?" Everyone looks a little confused, like they don't know what she's talking about. "Is that, like, a thing girls do? Ask boys for help with homework? Why wouldn't I just ask one of my friends?"

"It's just a way to get you to talk to him," Megan says, sounding like she's a professional love counselor.

Sunny sits up straight, almost like she's posing. "Okay." She takes a deep breath and lets it out. "No, I don't think I can do this, guys. Really."

"Why not?" I blurt out. I hate when Sunny gets like this.

"I don't know. He just won't like me. I know he won't. I couldn't even talk to him at Earth Club. It was like my mouth shut off," Sunny says.

For the rest of the night, we keep trying to convince her that she has a chance with Evan. But we're not having any luck so far.

Beauty tip: Worrying causes wrinkles. Make sure not
to scrunch up your forehead when stressed.

"Jane, I don't know if you think I'm kidding
about this, or if you're just not listening, but selling the house
may be the only way to stay in business." Grandma and Mom
are talking in the back office, but the door is open, so I can
hear them all the way at the front of the store, where I'm
reorganizing the stationery section. "It's practically the only
source of income we have."

There's a few seconds of silence, and then Mom says, "I
just don't think I can do that at this stage of my life. Live in
a tiny two-bedroom apartment above the store with you and
Lucy. I can't do that to my daughter."

Well, at least Mom's talking some sense now. No way
would I be able to live up there. Share a room with my mother?
Would we have bunk beds?

They start talking more quietly, so I move closer to

the office to hear them better. Then it almost sounds like they're laughing for a few minutes. I have no idea what brought that on.

"That or bankruptcy!" Grandma's voice is high at the end, almost singsong, like she's trying to make light of a horrible situation. She walks out of the office, and I pretend to be busy lining up pill bottles, but Grandma obviously knows I was listening, because she gives me that "I feel terrible" look and walks right by me without giving me any other jobs to do.

I keep up my busy-reorganizing attitude. I move on to fix up the toy section. For some reason, the noisiest toys are on the easiest-to-reach shelf. That makes no sense to me, since little kids are always touching them. So I decide to put the dolls and the board games on the lower shelves and all of the toy instruments and beeping, honking car toys on the top shelves.

I wonder what Sunny's doing now. Probably just lying on her bed, dreaming about Evan. Or maybe even watching that *Charlie Brown* DVD again.

Well, maybe I can't save the pharmacy overnight, but I think I can do something to help Sunny. I can ask Claudia for advice since she's already had three boyfriends. I could even ask Mom or Grandma for advice, because I feel like this is something they might know about.

But even better: I can use the pharmacy as a library! We have a pretty good selection too: *Cosmo, Redbook, Glamour.* All of those talk about getting a guy to like you, don't they? I've never actually read them, but I've reorganized the shelves, so I've seen the covers. Plus, Grandma gets all the teen magazines too, and those are filled with crush-snagging tips.

I feel good that I've found such a productive thing to do with my day. Helping Sunny is just as important as helping Mom and Grandma. No one can deny that.

And if I still have time when I'm done with my boy research for Sunny, I'll read another chapter in *The New Beauty Secrets: Your Ultimate Guide to a Flawless Face.* Laura Mercier wrote it. She's one of my idols.

There's a lot to admire about her. First of all, her goal is to accentuate a person's natural beauty through their makeup. That's my goal too. She has her own very successful makeup line, and she began her training as a makeup artist at seventeen. That's only five years away for me, and I've already started my training, even though it's not official.

I take a big stack of magazines and sit down in one of the plastic chairs. We have a makeshift area where people can wait for prescriptions, but people usually stand anyway. I don't get that. Why stand when you can sit? It's true what Mom says, that people are always in such a rush these days.

That's why no one sits at the counter anymore. Why no one orders Grandma's delicious grilled-cheese sandwiches anymore. Why our milk-shake maker was donated to the Jewish Community Center.

The pharmacy changes with the rest of society, I guess. I just wish it were different. It seems like the golden years of Old Mill Pharmacy were when I was six, seven, eight. I wonder if it will ever be like that again.

I wonder if I'm the only twelve-year-old in the world who thinks like this.

As I'm reading through the magazines, trying to find things for Sunny, I come across an interesting article: "Making Relaxation Space." It talks about devoting a corner of your house or office just to relaxation. It says you can put out candles, maybe even aromatherapy ones. You can have soft lighting and relaxing music playing too. "Make sure you steer clear of electronics," it says. "Do not have anything to distract from relaxation; make this a stress-free place."

As I'm reading, I realize that my butt is very sore from sitting on the flimsy plastic chair for so long. Maybe that's why people don't choose to sit here. Maybe they don't want to eat at the counter because it doesn't seem inviting.

Old Mill Pharmacy needs a Relaxation Room! A place where customers can go while they're waiting for prescriptions to be filled. A place that's quiet and peaceful. And we can keep the magazines there so people will actually read them and buy them!

This won't be an expensive thing, really, since the whole hunting section is empty anyway, and we have room for it. We could block it off, add some mood lighting, and we'd be set!

Maybe something like this could help get things back to the way they used to be.

11

Business tip: Ask yourself, what are your competitors doing that you aren't doing?

"**Mom!**" I jump up from the chair and run to the office with the magazine. "I have such an awesome idea!"

I know Mom's the person to go to for this kind of thing. She's usually open to people's ideas, plus she'll see the importance of something like this—she's always saying how everyone's too busy to relax and enjoy life.

When I walk into the pharmacy office, Mom's standing there talking to Tory and Charise, who came by to pick up their last paychecks. They're each holding two big shopping bags.

"Thank you so much, Jane," Tory says.

"Okay guys, go quick, before my mother sees you," Mom says. "Just kidding. She wouldn't mind that I'm giving you free stuff, because she loves you."

"Well, we really appreciate it," Charise says, and they both give my mom a hug.

"Mom," I say after Tory and Charise have left the office.

"Yes, Lucy?" she says, smiling at me.

"I have such a good idea for the store. Ready to hear it?"

"Lucy, you don't need to work so hard around here," she says. "You're still a kid."

"Mom." I roll my eyes at her. "I like helping!"

She smiles at me and pulls me into a hug. She gets this way sometimes, overemotional. Once she said it's because she doesn't want me to feel obligated to work here when I'm older—I should be free to pursue my passion, whatever that means. Sometimes she thinks too far into the future.

I pull back from the hug and say, "It's just an idea I have for the empty hunting section. Okay? So listen."

She nods.

"We need a Relaxation Room. We need to do it now."

Mom smiles and says, "Please explain."

"Here. Read this." I hand her the magazine, which I'd stuck under my armpit while we were hugging. "If we do this, maybe that part of the store won't look so depressing anymore."

I walk out of the office so Mom can read the article in peace, and I head over to the section that will soon be the new relaxation space. The one problem I see is a lack of comfortable seating. We need that. And I know Grandma won't let me buy couches or anything. I'll have to find a way around that—maybe ask for donations.

When I get like this, so excited about something, I can hardly contain myself. My words come quickly and my voice gets high-pitched, and it's like things just can't happen fast enough. I need it to happen now. I need it to have happened five minutes ago!

While Mom's reading, I decide to give Sunny a call and check in on her.

"Hey, Sun," I say. "Another fabulous Sunny sleepover."

"Totally. How's the pharmacy today?"

I plop back down in one of the plastic chairs. I'm about to tell Sunny all about the Relaxation Room and my plans when I suddenly realize it's too soon for that. I'm getting ahead of myself. "It's slow. Listen, I've been reading some magazines. Some *looooooove* magazines. And I have some advice for you."

"Lucy," Sunny groans, half-laughing, half-annoyed. "What kind of magazines have you been reading?"

"Just, y'know, like women's magazines, like *Cosmo* and stuff." I reach into my pocket for a piece of strawberry gum. "And I was right—the key to landing a man is confidence."

"Landing a man?" Sunny laughs again. "Lucy, we're twelve, not fifty."

"I know, I know." I pop a bubble and the gum lands all

69

over my face. It takes me a little while to get all of it off. "It's just an expression."

"Oh-kay."

"So, yeah, you're awesome. You should know that," I tell Sunny. I hear my name from the office. "But I gotta go—my mom's calling me. Talk to you later!"

"Lucy, you are my daughter, after all," Mom says, coming out of the office to squeeze me in a tight hug. "I knew it. We're cut from the same cloth. We have the same priorities."

Okay, now she's taking this too far.

"Mom, it's just a good idea—that's all." I smile at her, pulling back from the hug. Strands of her blonde hair are stuck to my blue T-shirt. "It's what we need. And the thing is, it won't really cost the pharmacy anything. It'll just add a level of ambience, like the article says," I tell her.

Mom says, "Yup. And it stresses the importance of mental rest, breaks from this work-work-work lifestyle the world has placed on us." She looks at me again, even more adoringly this time. "And we can take those denim couches out of the basement. I've been wanting to get rid of them anyway."

"Genius! That solves the seating problem," I tell her.

"Okay, go tell Grandma," Mom says, walking away from me.

"No, you tell Grandma."

Mom's bouncing up and down on her toes, all perky, like a little girl. "Lucy, she'll take it better from you. Trust me."

I flip my hair over, trying to adjust my elastic headband. "Mom . . ."

"Lucy . . ."

I sigh. "Fine. You're right. Grandma has a hard time saying no to me."

Beauty tip: Laughter is good for the body and the soul and also brings color to the cheeks.

"What?" Grandma asks. She's sitting behind the prescription counter, going through a stack of papers.

"Grandma, just take a break for one second. I want to tell you something."

Finally she puts the stack of papers down, leans her elbows on it, and looks up at me. "Yes, my dear?"

I pull over a stool and sit next to her. "So you know I've been trying really hard to think of ways to improve the pharmacy and stuff?"

She nods.

"This morning I was reading through magazines, and one article gave me a really, really, really good idea." I pause and smile at Grandma. "Ready?"

She nods again. Now she's smiling.

"The section where we used to have the hunting supplies should be turned into a Relaxation Room! It's already kind of blocked off, since you never liked hunting anyway. And it's really not an expensive thing to do. And Mom said I could take the couches in the basement. And—"

"Lucy." Grandma puts her hand on my shoulder. "Slow down. What exactly is a Relaxation Room?"

I try to slow down and explain it to her, emphasizing the fact that it won't really cost anything. Out of the corner of my eye, I see Mom walking over to us. She's carrying a brochure from her favorite magazine distributor.

"Luce, we need to subscribe to these *Body & Wellness* journals. They really focus on inner peace, relaxation, and stress-free living." She looks up from the brochure. "I've been wanting to stock these forever, but now we have a real reason!"

Grandma gives me a look. "I thought it wasn't going to cost us anything?"

"Well, I hadn't thought of subscribing to those magazines, but it's a really good idea because customers will feel even more relaxed reading that stuff."

Grandma's smiling again, and it's good to know that she can't resist my genius idea. It's good to know that Mom supports it too.

"No candles, though," Grandma says. "We can't risk burning the store down for a few people's feelings of calm."

"Fine, fine," I say. "Makes sense."

"But we can have some calm, serene music playing," Grandma says. "That'll work."

After Grandma okays the Relaxation Room, I head over to that space right away, just so that I can get a sense of how it should be organized.

"Um, Lucy?" I hear, and turn around.

Unfortunately, Erica Crane's standing there, sifting through her Louis Vuitton bag. She swears it's real, but I think it's a fake.

"Isn't it, like, illegal that your parents make you work here?" she asks. "'Cuz my uncle's a lawyer, and he could totally report your family."

I roll my eyes at her. "It's not illegal, Erica. Thanks for your concern."

"Hmm. I know what I'm talking about and—" Thankfully, her mother calls her from the front door of the pharmacy, saying she's leaving. Erica doesn't say good-bye, and I'm glad. I don't want to hear another word.

I spend the rest of the day cleaning out the hunting section, getting rid of paper and other stuff that has been cluttering up the space. It feels so good to actually be doing something, not just hoping and praying that something will happen.

It's the same feeling I got after I helped Courtney Adner for homecoming. And especially after she came back to tell me that I was her hero.

Maybe these things are pretty small, and they're not making the pharmacy billions of dollars or anything. But they are helping people. And that's what Grandma says is most important anyway.

When Grandma came to Old Mill Middle School last year for Professional Day, she gave the best speech. She told us why she became a pharmacist and why Grandpa became one too. She said it's the best job, because it's a way to be part of the community and to help people at the same time. I sat in the front row; Sunny sat next to me. And I was beaming, really and truly beaming. I was so proud of Grandma that day, but I guess I'm always proud of her. I'm proud of the way she helps people and loves it. And I'm really proud that even with business being bad, she's happy every single day to go to work.

I hope I'm like that when I'm older and have a real job.

13

Business tip: Make sure you have an organized filing system for bills and expenses.

"*Morrie, come on back,*" I hear Grandma say, and I don't like the sound of it.

Morrie is our accountant and financial adviser. He's an old friend of Grandpa's, and he's been with the store since the beginning. Grandma believes everything he says, so when she gets stressed and worried, she calls him in for guidance. The past few times Morrie has been here, Grandma was in a really bad mood when he left.

"Hello, Lucy," Morrie says when he gets to the office. "What're you working on?"

"Oh, just playing online," I say.

"Kids and the Internet, huh, Doris?" Morrie shakes his head. "My granddaughter Bevin spends hours and hours on the Internet, doing God knows what."

"Morrie, sit," Grandma says, pulling out a chair for

him. "I need you to give it to me straight. Please, none of your fancy talk—'if we do this, then maybe we can do that.' None of that. I need to know where we stand."

"Doris, I'll just—"

"Don't interrupt," Grandma says, leaning back in her desk chair. "I plan to talk to Flo, and get some comps from her, and put the house on the market eventually."

"All right, let's look at the numbers," Morrie says.

Grandma puts her hand on my shoulder. "Lucy, darling, can you fix up the skin-care aisle? It's really looking terrible."

It's obvious Grandma is trying to find a reason to kick me out. "Sure," I grumble.

"Jane, get in here," Grandma calls from the office doorway as I'm on my way out. There are a few people in the Relaxation Room, but they don't seem to be paying attention. I think they're just killing time before their movie starts.

The skin-care stuff is already organized, so I walk over to the office and crouch down behind the prescription counter. It's a good eavesdropping position; I can hear most everything, and no one can see me.

"Ma, can I talk to you for a second?" Mom asks before she walks into the office. "Alone?"

"Excuse me, Morrie." Grandma walks outside the office and closes the door.

"I don't want to talk to Morrie. He says the same thing every time. Gary this and Gary that. And I'm tired of him trying to set me up with his son," Mom says. "We went out once, and he wasn't my type. I wish he'd get over it!"

I'm kind of glad she says that. Because even though my dad moved to London when I was three years old and I only see him once a year now, my parents aren't legally divorced; they've just been separated for a really long time.

Deep down, I hope they'll get back together one day. I still have hope, because my dad still loves my mom. I know he does because he took her name when they got married instead of her taking his. That's a big deal, I think.

"Jane," Grandma says sharply, and I can see her shaking her head. "Get a grip. Morrie's not here to set you up with Gary. He's here to help us. What is wrong with you?"

"I'm just saying, Ma," Mom whispers. "I really don't—"

"Shhh! Shhh! Shhh!" Grandma shakes her head furiously and pulls Mom into the office.

"Sorry, Morrie," Grandma says. "Please, go on."

"First of all, looking toward the future a little, as far as I can tell, you're not going to have the money to pay your taxes this year," Morrie says. "And after I've accounted for everything, you probably won't be able to afford the mortgage payments on the store. That refinancing really hurt you. The bills are going to be a struggle too."

"So, you're saying . . ." Mom's voice trails off.

"Well, unless you win the lottery or inherit large sums of money from a mysterious relative," Morrie says, "you're really in danger. The pharmacy isn't bringing in enough to support your lifestyle, let alone cover the store's expenses."

"But there are loans, aren't there?" Mom asks. "I mean, just to get us back on our feet, maybe do some renovating?"

"Jane, I didn't bring you in here for ideas. I brought you in here so you'll know how grave the situation is," Grandma says loudly, and I'm pretty sure the women in the Relaxation Room can hear her now. But when I turn to see, the women have left.

"Okay, let's look at options," Morrie says. Even through the door, I can hear the nervousness in his voice. "Dor, you mentioned selling the house? The home mortgage is completely paid off, so that's a start."

"Wait," Mom says. "How much would we save if Claudia came home for a semester or two?"

There's a moment of silence, and then Morrie says, "Well, not so much, considering you're on a tuition payment plan and she has financial aid."

"So selling the house, moving into the apartment upstairs?" Grandma asks. "That's our best option, isn't it?"

Again, there's a break in the conversation. Finally, Morrie says, "Truthfully, it would be a Band-Aid on the situation. If things around here don't improve businesswise, you'll still run out of money eventually."

"What are you saying, Morrie?" Grandma asks.

"Maybe think of some ways to expand the store. Think of possible markets you haven't reached. People like to get many different items at one store, and you have the potential to offer that. You have a lot of unused space."

"Morrie, please," Grandma says, sounding more annoyed than before. "I don't have the time or the energy for such radical ideas."

No one says anything for a few seconds, and then Morrie says, "My son Gary's been sitting on a pile of money, not enough to live on for the rest of his life, but enough for now, from when he won all that money at the casino last summer. I know he would love to invest in something."

"Oh, Morrie," Mom says. "I don't think that's a good idea."

My mom is so freaked out about the possibility of getting forced to go on a date with Gary again. I wonder what happened when they did go out. It must have been really awful.

"Hmm." Morrie clears his throat. "If Gary lent you the money, it would just be a type of loan, you know. And Dor, a new way to expand the store doesn't have to be radical. It might be just waiting to present itself!"

Mom's been suggesting a health-food section for years, so that could be an idea. That's a way to expand. But would that really save the store?

I try to think of other ways we could expand, but it's just a weird thing to think about. How do you expand a store that's been around and been the same forever? We have the Relaxation Room, but it's not like we can make money from offering people a place to relax. After thinking for a few minutes, all I can come up with is that the grocery store does DVD rentals now. Maybe we could do that too.

All in all, though, no idea I can come up with seems very good. And besides, it would take a lot to convince Grandma to try something new.

Things are even worse than I thought.

14

Beauty tip: Dabbing a little concealer under
your eyes will brighten up your face.

At lunch a few days later, I'm telling
Sunny more about all those landing-a-man articles I read.
I'm determined to make her dream of Evan Mass a reality.

"Lucy, I really appreciate your help and everything, but
the thing is, we're talking about *me* here." Sunny moves her
chair closer to mine. "Let's face it, guys like Evan go out
with girls like Erica Crane. The nicest boys always go for
the meanest girls. It's just the way the world works."

She looks across the cafeteria to where he's sitting and
then quickly looks away. That's my cue to look over. We
try not to make our spying obvious. Evan Mass has thick,
black hair, and it's pin straight. His eyes are blue, so blue
they look almost fake, kind of like the blue part of a snow
cone.

I look back at Sunny, lowering my eyes to give her a
cold, hard stare. "Sunny, how do you know that?"

She shrugs. "I just do. Asha always tells me. It's easy for us to like American guys, but they don't always like us back."

I can't take much more of Sunny's negative thinking and talking. It's dumb, and it's annoying, and if she actually does think like this, then I don't need to listen to her going on and on about Evan Mass.

"We need a plan, Sunny," I tell her. "Action. We need to think of stuff you can talk to him about at Earth Club."

Sunny puts the back of her hand against my forehead and laughs. "Lucy Desberg, are you sick? What has gotten into you?"

I laugh too, but then I'm back to business. "C'mon, let's make a plan."

"Lucy," she groans. "Seriously, it's okay. Sometimes it's fun just to think about him and stare at him across the cafeteria."

I give her a look. "Really?" I pick a tater tot off of Sunny's lunch tray and pop it into my mouth.

Sunny rolls her lips together and gives me a pathetic look. "Kinda."

That's one of the major differences between Sunny and me. We're best friends and everything, but she likes to stay in dreamland, while I want to take a nonstop flight to reality and actually do something.

At Earth Club later, Sunny talks to Evan less than she did last time. I don't know how that's even possible, but it's true. I try to ignore how stupid she's being and focus on actual environmental stuff, though, since I *am* stuck in the club.

At least we're not collecting recyclables this time. Today we're researching what it would take to make Old Mill Middle School a green school. From what I'm reading, going green can actually be really simple. Like, instead of carrying our dirty gym clothes home in plastic bags, we could bring in cloth bags and reuse them. That's really easy! And every year at the Memorial Day Carnival, we could make sure that none of the kids let the balloons fly away. There are lots of little things like that.

"Since we're just beginning our research today, it might be good to look at green businesses as well," Mrs. Deleccio says to all of us. "Just to get an example of what all kinds of communities are doing. Think churches, apartment buildings, anything you can."

After she says that, I remember Claudia telling me about that eco-spa she went to for her birthday. That's the only green business I've ever heard of.

I wonder what kinds of green businesses there are in Connecticut, so I do a search and I find a Web site that lists all of the state's green businesses. There are green car dealerships that sell only hybrids. And there are green bakeries that sell only organic baked goods and have cork flooring and recycled wallpaper. It's kind of unbelievable that there are so many places like this out there, all of them doing their part to save the earth.

Then I do a search for green businesses nearby in Old Mill and Waterside and the surrounding towns. The first thing that comes up is our town Web site, OldMill.gov. I click on News from Mayor Danes, and a page with a letter from the mayor opens up.

Dear Old Mill Business Owners,

We are pleased to announce Old Mill's first Going Green Grant for local businesses. Have you been looking for a way to enhance your business? Do you care about the earth and want to preserve it? If so, this grant may be for you. Please read through the materials to see if your business qualifies. All applications are due by December 20th.

Good luck to all,
Mayor Phillip Danes

I finish looking through the page with the grant information; it seems really complicated. Like, you need all of this financial information and a whole business proposal. That letter from Mayor Danes makes it sound easy, but it's actually really hard.

"Lucy, did you hear me?"

I look up from the computer and see Sunny and Yamir standing over me. Is Earth Club over already? I didn't even realize.

"We gotta go," Yamir says. "Are you on another planet or something? Mrs. Deleccio dismissed us, like, two minutes ago."

I turn off the computer and follow them out to the parking lot, where Mrs. Ramal is waiting for us. I can't believe how much I just learned. It was like all of that green information just washed over me and I absorbed it.

Yamir and I are sitting in the backseat together again, and I move as close to the window as I can. I really don't want our thighs to touch again.

I wish Sunny would let him have the front seat once in a while.

Beauty tip: Make sure to blend your foundation and bronzer for an even, smooth tone.

Ever since I came up with the Relaxation Room idea, I've been pretty busy at the pharmacy. I'm always adjusting the lighting, making sure the couch cushions are neat, and generally making sure the room looks presentable. I want people to want to sit there.

It's a work in progress, and I know that. But it's really fun to work on it. And it's also bringing in business! Just yesterday a woman bought a few of the *Body & Wellness* journals. And last weekend, while a man was waiting for his prescriptions, he bought an iced tea and a bag of pretzels and enjoyed them in the Relaxation Room.

I'm putting up some posters, the kind that usually hang in a guidance counselor's office. They say things like: DREAM BIG! and CLIMB HIGHER!

Maybe they aren't the most beautiful pieces of art in the world, but I like them, and I think they're inspiring. And, most important, they were free. Meredith Ganzi's aunt is a guidance counselor, and she was redecorating her office, so Meredith brought them in for me. Meredith can be really thoughtful sometimes.

"Is Lucy here?" I hear someone ask from the front of the store. I turn around to see who it is.

"Hi, Cassandra!" I call from inside the Relaxation Room. Aside from Sunny, Cassandra's the friend of mine who visits the pharmacy the most. Her mom has always been a loyal customer. "Come check this out!"

When Cassandra gets to the Relaxation Room, she looks around, confused. I should have known I'd need to explain this to her.

"It's a Relaxation Room," I tell her. "When people are waiting for prescriptions, they can just sit in a quiet place. And maybe it'll really catch on, and people will come here just to relax!"

"Good idea, Lucy," Cassandra says. "It's really cool."

"So, do you need help with anything?" I ask. Cassandra's still just looking around the room like she's never seen anything quite like it.

"I'm here with my mom and sister. My sister's been begging

for makeup, and she has a sweet sixteen to go to soon, so my mom finally gave in."

I walk out of the Relaxation Room, and Cassandra follows me. "Well, I can give suggestions," I say, feeling excited about another potential makeover.

"Oh yeah," Cassandra says, giggling. "I forgot you're, like, Ms. Maybelline."

Cassandra's mom and sister, Kristin, are in the makeup section of the store. "Mom, you have no idea what kind of makeup girls my age wear, okay?" Kristin says to their mother. "So stop trying to butt in."

"Can I help you guys?" I ask them, smiling as sweetly as possible. I have a way with grown-ups. They usually really like me.

Kristin gives me a dirty look, though. I may get along with grown-ups, but definitely not with older sisters.

"Hi, Lucy," Cassandra's mom says, readjusting her pocketbook on her shoulder. "We're trying to find some respectable"—she shoots Kristin a look—"makeup for Kristin."

"Mom. Can you please stop?" Kristin folds her arms across her chest and looks away from her mother, examining the black and burgundy shades of nail polish. Kristin's not really one of those black-is-the-only-color kind of girls, but I can tell she's an I-like-to-stress-my-mother-out kind of girl.

"I can help," I say, not even looking at Kristin to see what kind of face she makes at me. "I know every single product we have. And we also have another makeup line, called Earth Beauty, that's near the prescription counter."

"Earth Beauty?" Kristin asks, with one nostril flared. Her highlights are almost grown out, and her hair is black on top and blonde on the bottom.

"It just means the products aren't tested on animals. It's actually a really popular line." Okay, a tiny white lie. I pause, giving her time to think about it. I'm debating saying something else about the Earth Beauty line, something true. And even though I know I shouldn't gossip, I do it anyway. "Courtney Adner is a big fan of their chemical rinse."

Kristin's cheeks turn red, and when she speaks her voice is scratchy. "She is?"

I nod. Courtney Adner is a year older than Kristin. But I knew Kristin would care about what kinds of products Courtney uses. Courtney Adner just has that effect on people. "Okay, so let's test the blush colors here, and then we'll go to Earth Beauty for the lipsticks and mascaras. Those are their best products."

"Cassandra, does she know what she's talking about?" Kristin whispers, loud enough for me to hear.

"Definitely. She's, like, an owner of the pharmacy."

Cassandra may not be Mrs. Einstein, but she's helpful at times like this.

"We'd love some help, sweetie," Cassandra's mom says to me.

I show them all of the tester products we have so they don't go and start opening every package just to see the color. People have done that before, and it's rude and wasteful. Don't they know we can't sell those products afterward?

It takes a really long time, but finally Kristin seems happy with her choices. Well, as happy as Kristin can be. She's decided on a blush, a bronzer, two eye shadows, eyeliner, mascara, and a few lip balms and lipsticks.

When Kristin and her mom are heading to the register, Cassandra turns to me and whispers, "She tries to act all cool. But she has no idea how to put on makeup. And none of her friends even care about that stuff."

"Really?" I ask.

"Oh yeah. My sister's, like, desperately trying to be in the popular group, but she's totally failing. She cries about it every night. And I stole her journal, and she's already filled up sixty pages just on that."

"Really?" I ask again.

"Uh-huh," Cassandra replies, sounding almost happy

about this fact. "And it's not even her friend's sweet sixteen that's coming up. It's Laura Gregory's, and she invited the whole grade. My sister is so happy she gets to go, though. But she knows she needs to look good because it's Laura Gregory, my sister's idol." Cassandra laughs at that, then she takes a bag of Twizzlers off the shelf, opens it, and eats a few.

She'd better pay for that, but there's no time to worry about the Twizzlers now; I need to help Kristin. She may be kind of a pain, but I can't let her go to Laura Gregory's sweet sixteen with really bad makeup.

It's clear her mom has absolutely no idea about this stuff. Her eyebrows look like they've never been tweezed in her whole entire life, and she has turquoise eye shadow on, the color you'd wear if you were in a play about mermaids.

"Hey, Kristin," I call. Kristin and her mom are standing by the office, talking to my mother. I'm sure they're discussing stupid PTA stuff. Kristin looks bored to tears.

Kristin turns around, and I run up to her.

"I know how to do makeup, you know," I tell her. "My sister, Claudia, and I have been practicing on each other for years now. It's my passion. I am going to be Laura Mercier when I grow up."

"Oh, I know your sister." Kristin smiles. "She was president of Support the Arts last year. She's so nice."

I smile. Cassandra was right—Kristin's popular-girl-obsessed. I'll have to tell Claudia how helpful she was in breaking the tension. "I can do your makeup for the sweet sixteen, if you want."

Kristin looks down at the floor, picking at her cuticles. "I doubt my mom will pay for that. She really doesn't want me to wear makeup. I'm paying for this stuff out of my birthday money."

I laugh. Does Kristin really think I'd charge? I'm a twelve-year-old makeup artist.

"Oh, it's free," I say. "No one should ever charge to do makeup. Even fancy spas don't charge—they just expect you to buy the products after. But you already have the products!"

Kristin smiles and starts chewing on her pinky nail, thinking it over, I guess. "Yeah, actually, that'd be really awesome," she says. "I'm sure if you and Claudia practiced together, you're really good at it. Claudia always looked so pretty—natural pretty, though. She didn't even wear that much makeup. Just, like, the perfect amount."

"Oh yeah, don't worry." I smile and look over at her mom and my mom chatting like they've known each other for years. "Claudia taught me everything I know."

Kristin and I make a makeup application date, and then she goes back to her mom so they can pay for the stuff. I look around and realize I've somehow lost Cassandra, but a few minutes later, I find her in the Relaxation Room. She's sprawled out on the couch with the empty bag of Twizzlers next to her.

"This place is really relaxing," she says, sounding half-asleep.

"Good! But listen, Cass, your mom and sister are leaving the store now. And if you stay here, my grandma's gonna put you to work."

She jumps up from one of the denim couches, and when she realizes she never paid for the bag of Twizzlers, she gives me a confused, sorry, "what should I do now?" look.

"Don't worry about it," I say, taking the package from her and putting it in my pocket. "But next time you're paying."

Cassandra smiles and leaves the store. I'm already excited about doing Kristin's makeup. I hope Mom and Grandma won't think that's really weird or inappropriate. But they shouldn't. There's nothing wrong with it.

And look at the difference it's already made in Kristin's life. When she walked into the store she was angry and miserable, and when she left she was more relaxed, happier, even a little more confident.

I don't like it when people say makeup makes you prettier. That's not really true. Makeup *can* make you feel a little better about yourself, though. Like when you've broken out but you have the perfect shade of concealer, you don't feel as upset about going to school. You feel okay about yourself. And then you carry yourself better and smile more—you're generally happier.

When I tell my friends this kind of stuff, they think I'm crazy. They think I talk like a psychologist or something; that's what Sunny says. I can't help it, though, if these kinds of things are ingrained in me. I can't help it if this is the business I was born into.

16

Beauty tip: Make sure to get your beauty sleep.

"*Flo, I want you to tell me,* ballpark, what this house will go for," Grandma says. I'm still in bed, all cozy under my down comforter, with the sun streaming in through the windows.

"Flo, ballpark," Grandma says again. "The most you think we can get for it. The least you think we can get for it."

I hate it when Grandma calls her Flo. It sounds so gross.

I just woke up, and I was in a good mood too, because it's parent-teacher conference day. And that means no school. But waking up to Grandma on the phone with her friend Florence has squashed my good mood like a sneaker on an ant.

Normally, Grandma on the phone with Florence wouldn't faze me at all, but today it does. Florence is a real estate agent, and it's very obvious what they're talking about, especially since I overheard Grandma's conversation with Morrie the other day.

Instead of staying in bed for a few minutes longer, I walk into the computer room to see if I can find out anything more about Mayor Danes's grant. I've been thinking about it, and maybe it's not as hard as I originally imagined. Maybe I just need to read the application over more carefully.

I go straight to OldMill.gov and then click to bring up the News from Mayor Danes page.

The grant application opens up as a PDF, and when I scroll through it, I see that it's twenty-eight pages long! A lot of that is instructions and guidelines, but still—that's a lot to read in one sitting.

I print it out, go back to my room, and put it on my desk. I'll read through it later. The real problem is, I'm not really sure this is something I can do on my own, and I don't want to add another thing to stress Grandma out.

It's probably not even worth it, anyway. I'm sure a lot of businesses are trying for it.

The house has been silent for a few minutes, and I wonder if Grandma's off the phone with Flo. I slump down the stairs, still in my pajamas.

Grandma's still on the phone, but she sees me, waves, and then starts doodling on the memo pad in front of her. I pour myself a bowl of Crispix, cut up a banana, and sit down in the den to eat my breakfast. Flo doesn't seem to be letting

Grandma get a word in. I turn on the TV so Grandma won't think I'm listening.

"That's great. Actually, just hearing this from you has made me feel better," Grandma says finally. "I want to be able to stay in business without worrying every day, and having the money from the sale of the house will help."

I take another bite of Crispix, trying to crunch as softly as possible. But I don't know how I'm able to eat at a time like this. Grandma's serious about selling this house. "Flo, I'm not concerned about what Jane will say!" Grandma yells into the phone. Florence is that kind of friend—the kind you can yell at and not worry about it. "We have Claudia's college to pay for, and Lucy's eventually. It's got to be done."

Through the entryway to the kitchen, I can see Grandma pacing. "I don't have other options, Flo," Grandma says, more quietly now. "Unless you count going out of business. That's hardly an option. Jane and I will end up killing each other. Besides, can you imagine me folding shirts at the Gap?"

I burst out laughing. Milk and Crispix fly out of my mouth and land on the glass coffee table. This is really no time for laughing, but I can't help it.

"All right, Flo, we'll talk later about when to list it and all of that," Grandma says, sounding calmer now. "Get me some comps, and call me later. Love to Bernie."

Grandma gets off the phone and sits down at the kitchen table. She puts her head down, and I don't know if I should go in there and talk to her, acknowledging that I just heard that whole conversation, or if I should just go up to my room and call Sunny and figure out what time she's coming over.

I'm still sitting on the couch thinking this over when I see Grandma standing in the doorway to the den.

"You heard?" she asks.

I nod.

"I don't want to do this, Lucy, but I can't take this constant worry anymore." She comes to sit down next to me, and I rest my head on her shoulder.

"Grandma, I can't believe you. You don't even listen to your own advice," I say. "What do you tell everyone who comes into the pharmacy when they're worried about something? What do you tell me when I'm scared about a test?"

Grandma smiles. "What?"

I roll my eyes. "'Have a little faith, will ya?' That's what you always say."

Grandma's gray hair is tied back in a short little ponytail. I don't know any other grandmas who wear their hair this way. I like that she has long enough hair to do that, though. I like that she doesn't have boring, white, grandma hair.

"I know, Luce, I know." Grandma picks my bowl up off

the coffee table and stands up. "And I do have faith. I have faith that the business will pick up again, but until then, we need some extra money."

I follow her out of the den. "If we sell this house, we'll never get it back, you know," I say. "The maple tree that Grandpa planted in the front yard will be somebody else's. And the pool with fake rocks on the bottom—some other girl will be using it, inviting all of her friends over to go down the spiral slide a million times."

She doesn't respond to that, which I take as a good sign because maybe it means she's thinking it over, and maybe she's realizing that I'm right. That we can't sell this house.

I go up to my room to figure out what I'm wearing today.

A few minutes later, Grandma yells to me from downstairs. "Bye, Lucy, I'm heading over to the pharmacy."

Part of me feels guilty for not going to the pharmacy today to help out. But it's a school holiday, a day off, plus Sunny and I always hang out on school conference days. It's like a ritual.

Rituals shouldn't be broken. Not if it can be helped.

17

Beauty tip: The mall is a social fishbowl.
It's important to always look your best—no sweats!

"**We're going to the mall,**" Sunny says when she gets to my house. "I overheard Evan and his friends on the bus line yesterday. That's what they're doing today."

I'm so excited that Sunny's talking like this that I reach over and hug her, and we start jumping up and down together. "Good. I need to buy new sneakers anyway. And guess what?"

"What?"

"My mom didn't have any cash, so she left me her credit card!" I take it out from my jeans pocket and put it right up to Sunny's nose. "Cool, huh?"

She nods. "We're not gonna talk to the boys, though," Sunny says. "We can just watch them from afar. Oh, and we need code names."

"For ourselves?"

"No, dummy, for Evan and his friends. Just in case they overhear us." Sunny gets glasses out from the cabinet and pours us some fruit punch.

"Good idea, Sun."

"Evan's 'Cinnamon,'" she says. "We'll figure out the other code names when we see who he's with." She takes a sip of fruit punch. "My mom can drive us to the mall, because Yamir and his friends are going too. She just had to make a few stops, and she'll be back to get us."

"Yamir's coming with us?"

"Well, yeah. In the car."

"Oh, uh, okay." Ever since I sat alone with him in the backseat when he had that model of the earth, I feel all squirmy around him, like I don't want to get too close. Like everything will explode if we accidentally touch.

"So come on, let's get ready," Sunny declares. We take our juice up to my room. Sunny looks at herself in the full-length mirror.

"Is my outfit okay?"

I step back a little so I can get a good look. She's looking especially cute today in her dark jeans and her velvety green top. "Yeah, you look really cute. Want me to do your makeup for you?"

Sunny makes a face at me like she's sick of this question.

Ever since I helped Courtney with her hair trauma, I've been itching to give someone a makeover.

"Come on, Sun. Just a little blush. And some Pink Lollipop lip-gloss. I am so obsessed with it. It smells delicious! And let me dab some of that glitter eye shadow on your lids."

She immediately moves her hand to rub her eye. "No, I don't want to wear that stuff."

"It'll be so pretty, Sunny. It'll be like your eyes are dressed up!" I move closer to her. "Did I tell you I'm doing Cassandra's sister's makeup?"

"No." She looks away from the mirror and back at me. "Do you really think I need makeup?"

I sigh, loudly. "No, you don't *need* it. I've told you that a million times. You're so pretty naturally that it'd just be a finishing touch." I smile at her. "Don't be weird."

She flops herself down on her back on my bed. "You're the weird one. You're, like, super tense and angry all the time lately."

Now, I know that's not true. And even if it is a tiny bit true, maybe Sunny should understand why. I mean, my family is practically bankrupt. But Sunny's also going through a hard time. Having a crush isn't easy; I saw what it did to Claudia once, when she was into this guy Barry. I try to keep that in mind instead of getting mad.

"When's your mom getting here?" I ask, to change the subject.

"When she's done buying her products at *your* pharmacy," Sunny says, getting up from the bed. She starts pacing around my room. "Hey, what's this?" She picks the grant application up off my desk. "Going Green Grant?"

Sunny and I are so close that we never worry about looking through each other's stuff. I probably should've hidden the grant, though, because now it's going to take forever to explain. "Oh, I found it the other day at Earth Club when we were researching green businesses online." I take another look at myself in my full-length mirror. I can't wait for my new sneakers! They are going to look amazing with the jeans I'm wearing.

"The print is so small. It's like you need a PhD to understand it."

I laugh. "I know. I probably won't bother with it. We don't have that much time, and it's, like, written in a foreign language. I can't bug my mom and grandma with that now."

She shrugs. "Yeah, if it was something for kids, Mrs. Deleccio would have told us about it. Don't ya think?"

"You're probably right. She knows everything earthy going on around here," I say. "Let's go wait for your mom." We go downstairs, and Sunny asks me seven times if I think that

Evan will ever like her. Every time, I say yes. Truth is, I don't know Evan Mass that well. But I do know Sunny, and she's very likable.

I wish she could just relax and talk to him like a normal person. Then who knows what could happen?

18

Don't be afraid to dream and experiment.

—*Laura Mercier*

𝒯*he ride to the mall* is just as bad as I thought it'd be. Yamir and his friends Clint and Anthony put their sweaty faces against the car windows and then comment that the imprints of their cheeks on the windows look like butts.

At the mall, Sunny and I make our first stop at the food court. We do this for two reasons. One, it's a place where we can hang out and no one will think we're stalkers or weirdos. Two—which is obvious—we're hungry! We get pizza and Chinese food, and we share both. And afterward, we get frozen custard for dessert.

The food's fine and everything, but so far we haven't seen Evan at all. I'm not worried, though. We still have a while.

"Where do you think Evan shops?" Sunny asks me gloomily.

I shake my head at her. "Sun, I don't think he really shops. I think he just hangs out."

"Really?"

I don't understand Sunny's surprise. Did she really think that seventh-grade boys like to shop? "Come on." I grab her hand and pull her. "We gotta go buy my sneaks."

"What kind of sneakers are you gonna get?" she asks me. She's already asked me this three times today. Her mind is obviously somewhere else.

"Navy Converse. I told you that," I say as we're walking into Sneaker Shack.

She shrugs.

"Can I help you two?" a young guy, probably about twenty-two, asks us.

"I'd like navy Converse, the low-tops, in a size five," I tell him.

"Wow. You're a girl who knows what she wants," the guy says, laughing. "I'll be right back."

He's right; I *am* a girl who knows what she wants, and not only when it comes to sneakers. But knowing you want new sneakers and then getting them is pretty easy. Knowing you want to save your family business might be easy, but actually saving it is far from it.

I'm a lot like my mom when it comes to determination.

But sometimes my mom's determination gets in the way of her seeing reality. And my grandma is kind of the opposite. She's too realistic, and that gets in the way of her having any kind of drive to make a change.

I think I'm a good combination of both.

As we're waiting for the guy to come back, Sunny and I sit on the store's seats that are made to look like bleachers, like we're at a real game. I'm trying to nonchalantly stare out the store window and look for Evan. No sign of him so far.

"I brought two sizes," the sneaker man says. "Five, and five and a half. Just in case."

"Oh, thanks, but I know I need the five," I tell him. "I tried them on last week at Athlete Zone, but I'd rather buy them here."

The sneaker man gives me a confused look, like he has no idea what I'm talking about. I thought he'd be happy that I'm supporting the independent store. Oh well. "Follow me to the register, and you'll be all set," he says.

I am so excited about these sneakers. Getting new sneakers is making a big change in your life, getting a fresh start. That's why everyone gets new sneakers for the new school year, I think.

New sneakers change the outfits you choose to wear, because you want to wear stuff that goes with them. New sneakers are like a whole new beginning. I'll look at them, and they'll be all clean and new and perfect, and I think seeing them will empower me. Who knows, maybe they'll even help me have a better perspective on everything at the pharmacy. I know they're just sneakers, but a new beginning is a new beginning, even if it's just a new beginning for your feet.

I wish my mom and grandma could have something like this. Something to give them a new outlook, a new way to see our pharmacy and the influence it has on our community.

Maybe we all just need new Converse. Maybe it's simpler than we realize.

"That'll be forty-five sixty-three," he says. "I gave you the student discount."

I hand him the card. "Here ya go," I say, sounding like Grandma.

He goes to the back to run it through the credit card machine. I turn to Sunny and say, "I bet we're gonna see the boys right after this. I bet you they went to the video game store right around the corner."

"Maybe." Sunny shrugs, not sounding worried about whether we see the boys or not.

"Um," the sneaker man says when he gets back. "Hmmm. The card didn't work."

"Oh, I have a signed note that I have permission to use it.

But if you still need more evidence, the credit card company has my name on file."

He straightens his glasses and looks down at the card. "No, I believe you. But the card was actually declined," the man says. For the first time I notice he has the most nasal voice I've ever heard. And he's so skinny I really can't imagine him playing any sport, so it's funny that he works in a sneaker store.

I turn to look at Sunny, and she raises her shoulders like her neck is shrinking. She looks squirmy and uncomfortable. I can't believe this is happening right now. In front of Sunny, at the mall.

"Well, um, try it again," I say, smiling confidently. "I bet it was, like, a mistake." Out of the corner of my eye, I see Marnie Kastman browsing in the tennis section. If Marnie Kastman's here, then Erica Crane isn't too far away. Oh God, no. Why do they have to be here right now? And why does this have to happen to me in the first place? My mom's not even here to handle it.

Having your credit card declined is like writing on your forehead that your family doesn't have any money.

"Sorry, I tried it five times," he says, even more nasal now than before. "Why don't you come back with your mom later, okay? I'll hold these for you."

My chest is getting tight, and my whole body is starting to feel like a boiling pot of chicken soup. "I can't come back later. My mom's at work. And I really want these sneakers," I whisper, so Marnie doesn't hear me. I wish this guy could realize how important these sneakers are.

"Don't worry. I promise I'll hold them. I'll even hold them until next week," he says. "Really. They won't go anywhere."

"Um, well." I look over at my beautiful sneakers on the counter, so clean and perfect in their cardboard box. I bet Marnie and Erica are gonna get new sneakers today, wear them tomorrow, and I'll still be wearing my ratty old New Balances. "Okay. Thanks," I mumble.

"Sorry, Lucy," Sunny says, putting her arm around me as we leave the store. "But don't worry. You'll still get them."

"Yeah." But this is way more devastating than just missing out on a pair of new sneakers. It feels like all the prospects of a new beginning just melted away and are now sitting on the mall floor, ready to be mopped up and thrown in the garbage. There's no new start for me, no fresh addition to my wardrobe.

What if that's exactly what happens to the pharmacy too? Maybe being hopeful about small things like the Relaxation Room is a complete waste, because the potential for things to get better can disappear in a matter of seconds. I look at Sunny. I can't tell her any of this; she just wouldn't understand.

I take my cell phone out of my jeans pocket and dial Mom's cell.

No answer. Next, I try the pharmacy.

"Mom!" I exclaim as soon as she answers. "The credit card was declined. Again."

"Lucy, oh, there must be something wrong with Mastercard's computer system again. I'll call them. Okay?"

"Mom, I need those sneakers," I plead. "You promised. Remember?"

"Lucy, not now, please. I have stuff to do. We'll discuss this later. I love you." She hangs up before I even have a chance to say "I love you" back. Not that I even feel like saying it right now.

Sunny doesn't know what it's like for a credit card to be declined. I bet that's never even happened to her ever, or to her parents. But it happened to me today. And it happened to Mom last week at the grocery store. How horrible is that? Like, we don't even have enough money to eat? Now that's embarrassing.

For a few minutes I feel horrible. What exactly happens when a credit card gets declined? Will we get in trouble? All of these worries are swirling around in my head, but then I force myself to put those feelings away. We're here to find Evan, and I need to be a good friend. Being depressed about the stupid sneakers and the stupid credit card isn't going to make me feel better anyway.

"Maybe it's a sign that I shouldn't get Converse for seventh grade," I tell Sunny. When things like this happen, I always need to find a way to make sense of them. "Maybe I should get something different, like Asics, something no one else has."

"Maybe." She smiles.

"Or maybe—" Right there, right in the middle of the west wing of Waterview Mall, right as we're walking past the store where Sunny and I got our ears pierced in third grade, we spot Evan.

"There he is. There he is! Cinnamon!" Sunny says through clenched teeth. She grabs my hand and practically falls to the floor, dragging me down with her.

"Okay, shh! Come on." I take her hand, and we walk slowly to the benches right outside of Mommy-to-Be Maternity. We scooch down next to one of the benches, and I hand Sunny a mall directory pamphlet so we can pretend to be reading.

"Read," I say to Sunny.

"Who's he here with?" she asks. Her teeth are clenched so tight I'm worried they're going to crack in half.

"I can't see. Give me a second."

I peer out and over the bench a little so I can see Evan and his friends. He's with the twins Tyler and Brent, and also Tim and Wade.

I tell Sunny, and she immediately says, "Let's go home. Come on, I'll call Yamir on his cell, and we'll call my mom. I don't want to stay here anymore."

"Sunny, why?" I ask, confused.

"I don't want to see him. He's gross."

I lower my eyes and glare at her. "He is so not gross."

"Please, Lucy. Please," she says. "I don't think I like him anymore. And I can feel my skin breaking out right now from the stress."

"How can you say that?" I ask, ignoring her breakout comment. "We came here today to see him. You wanted to come here. You made up a code name. Remember?"

"Yeah, but I don't want to anymore," she whines. "Really, I don't even know why I like him."

"We came here, and we're going to talk to them," I declare. "Seriously. Stop being like this." Maybe I'm being too harsh with her, but there's no point in her acting like this. It's just stupid.

She says, "Let's just get up and pretend we didn't even see them. We'll walk away, do some browsing at Saks, of course check out the Laura Mercier counter before we leave, and we'll see if we can find Yamir." She looks at me, almost begging. "How about that?"

"Fine, but I'm not pleased," I say. I suddenly remind myself of my grandma—eerie.

Sunny gets up slowly, and we walk away from the bench with our backs toward Evan and his friends. Sunny seems more relaxed. All I want to do is go home. She's being so annoying.

Then we hear boys calling our names.

"Sunny Ramal! Lucy Desberg!"

I turn to look at Sunny, and I notice her dark skin turning red. Very, very red.

"You turn around first," she insists.

So I do. Evan and the boys are standing with their arms folded across their chests.

"Hi, guys," I say as confidently as I can, trying to act the way Claudia always does around guys.

"What're you up to?" Tyler, one of the twins, asks us.

"Just hanging out," I say. I nudge Sunny discreetly to get her to speak up, but so far she's saying nothing. Her facial expression is still one of shock, and her cheeks are still as red as a bad sunburn.

"I'm about to go beat these fine men at laser tag," Evan says, laughing.

"I'm awesome at laser tag." I nudge Sunny again, slightly harder, because this is actually a chance to hang out with Evan outside of Earth Club. Plus, we like laser tag. And Sunny is good at it, since Yamir's had a laser-tag birthday party for five years in a row. If she's not going to take action, then I'm gonna have to do it for her. "Sunny's even better."

"No, I'm not. Well, I used to be. Not anymore," Sunny mumbles.

"You're *so* good, Sunny. Shut up." I laugh, hoping it'll break the tension.

"Sunny, I know you can play laser tag," Evan says. "I was at Yamir's party a few years ago, when we were on the same soccer team." He smiles at Sunny and me. "And I remember that you were on my team. And we beat the crap out of Yamir's side!"

Sunny folds her arms across her chest. "Beginner's luck."

"If you guys play, and you beat us, we'll buy you pizza," Evan adds, cracking his knuckles. "How 'bout that?"

"I love pizza," I say. I can't even believe this is happening. And Sunny's just standing there. "Especially with extra cheese."

"Seriously, I have to go home," Sunny says. "Sorry. Come on, Lucy."

Evan shrugs. "All right. See ya."

The boys walk ahead of us, and I turn to look at Sunny.

She plops herself down on the mall floor, sitting with her head practically in her lap.

"Sunny, what was that?" I ask.

"I'm not playing laser tag with Evan Mass and his friends. That's, like, such a non girly thing to do," she says, and turns away from me.

"You're mad at me now?" I ask, talking to her back. "There's no reason for you to be mad at me. They invited us. And you just said no."

She doesn't respond.

"I was trying to help you." I get up and walk around so I can look at her. But she turns away again. "Sunny, you're being such a baby." I give her one last chance to say something, but she doesn't. "Fine, you said you wanted to leave, so let's leave."

There's no point in staying here anymore. I didn't get my sneakers, and Sunny doesn't even really want to hang out with Evan. I thought I'd maybe sneak a few Laura Mercier lipglosses onto my mom's credit card, but there's no chance of that happening now.

I fold my arms across my chest and stare at her. "Are you coming?"

She nods, puts her hands down on the mall floor, and gets up. "Sorry," she says.

"You better be." I roll my eyes at her. "But seriously,

Sunny, he wanted to hang out with you! Don't you realize that?"

"I don't know," she says quietly. "I guess so."

I grab her hand and guide her toward the Sephora. Then I put her right in front of one of their little stand-up mirrors. "See how pretty you are?" I ask, standing behind her.

"Lucy," she groans. "Stop. You sound like my mother."

"Your mom's pretty smart, and usually right."

Sunny shakes her head and rolls her eyes at me like I'm crazy, and we walk out of the store. "I can't wait until we're older and you have your own makeup line and it's sold in Sephora," she says, trying to change the subject.

"Don't rush." I smile. "I have a lot to do before that can happen!"

The credit card disaster made me realize now, more than ever, how dire the pharmacy's financial situation is. And Sunny has reminded me—I do have a lot to do. I really need to look at that grant application again; maybe I can figure it out this time.

Maybe it's just what we need to stay in business.

But I also realize something else. Why is the mall always the hangout? It's not so great—the benches aren't even that comfortable, and they're usually taken. And the food in the food court is pretty mediocre. Plus, there's no personal touch in any of the stores.

What if the pharmacy was the hangout instead of the mall? It used to be a hangout back in the day. We still have the grill, the soda fountain, the stools, and now we also have the Relaxation Room. It's easy to walk to, unlike the mall, and it's perfect for kids, because its not like a restaurant or bar.

If the pharmacy were a local meeting spot, a place where people felt comfortable sitting and staying for a few hours, it would definitely help business!

As we're walking out of the mall, I notice that Sunny's smiling. I think she feels a little bit better about herself now.

And that makes me feel better too.

19

Balance is the key to a beautifully made-up face.
—*Laura Mercier*

I'm in the Relaxation Room tidying up, rearranging the magazines, and waiting for Kristin to get here for her makeup application. I realize that I don't really have the perfect place to do her makeup. There's no tall chair or special mirror or even a good place to put the products. Since the pharmacy is quiet today, though, I figure I can use the Relaxation Room as my makeup artistry space. It's not like getting your makeup done is very stressful anyway. It kind of fits with the relaxation theme.

And after I'm done with Kristin's makeup, I'm going to sit down in the Relaxation Room and get some work done on the grant, or at least try to. I don't want to put it off any longer. I feel like the credit card getting declined was a sign that I need to really work hard to get things done. I found the grant application online that day for a reason; now I have to make it happen.

I can't just forget about it because it seems hard.

"I'm *heeeeeere*," Kristin says, more cheerful than I've ever seen her in the four years that I've known Cassandra. "And I brought my friend Erin with me. So she can see how it's done."

"Hi, um, sit down." I've propped a whole bunch of pillows up on the side of the couch so Kristin will be high enough. Also, I've turned on some more lights. I know that doesn't totally go with relaxation, but it's necessary.

"Erin, if you want your makeup done too, I have time," I say, trying as hard as I can not to laugh, because of course I have time! What else do I have to do?

"Not today, but maybe in a few weeks. We have another sweet sixteen coming up, and a *Quin-sin-eera*, or however you pronounce it!" She laughs, almost snorting. "I take French, not Spanish!"

Kristin hands me all of the makeup that she purchased the other day, and in my head, I start trying to figure out the best way to do this. She didn't buy any foundation, and she doesn't need it. However, she did buy powder, and that'll be the perfect way to blend her skin, making it all the same color.

"First I'm going to wash your face, okay?" Claudia taught me how important it is for your face to be clean before you put makeup on. "I'm just gonna use one of these Insta-facials."

After that, I apply the powder, and then the blush.

I take a break to show Kristin how she looks so far, in one of the makeup mirrors we sell by the front of the store. "What do you think?"

"Oh my God, I look, like, put together," Kristin says, turning to Erin. "Right?"

Erin shrugs. "I guess?"

I tap Kristin on the shoulder so that she'll turn back around and face me. "Okay, now it's time for the eyes." I put some foundation eye shadow on first, to create an even base color. Then I apply the pale pink shadow she bought, with a little of the charcoal gray shadow in the creases.

After that, all that's left is the lipstick, and it's too early for that. "I'm not gonna do the lipstick now," I tell her. "It'll rub off way before it's time for the party. And then your lips will be kind of stained and stuff. It's better to wait."

Kristin nods like she'd believe anything I said.

"So are you ready for a look at the final product?" I glance over at Erin to get a sense of what Kristin's reaction is going to be. I figure if Erin looks impressed, Kristin will too. But unfortunately, Erin looks horrified. Her hand is over her mouth, and she has a mushed-up, distorted kind of expression on her face.

I'm ready for Kristin to yell out an emphatic *yes!* but

sadly she does the same thing I did and turns to look at Erin.

"What?" Kristin asks Erin, sounding suddenly on the verge of tears. "What? Tell me."

Erin tightens her face, making it look like a dried-up prune. "It's just . . . um . . . It's just . . ."

"It's just *what*?" Kristin yells. "*What*, Erin?"

"You look, so, I don't know. So, like, mature, and grown-up, and adultish."

I hand Kristin the mirror, and that's when her jaw drops and her cheeks get red, natural red, in addition to the pinkness of the blush.

"I love it!" Kristin jumps up from the pillows, puts down the mirror, and reaches out to hug me like I've just given her one of those big checks from Publishers Clearing House.

"Lucy, you are a makeup goddess. A genius. You have made me feel so much better. I'll go tonight, and even if my royal blue dress is cheesy and lame, I'll look good anyway."

"Kristin, I was the one who suggested you get that royal blue dress," Erin says.

"Yeah, and I do like it. Just not as much as this makeup!" Kristin hugs me again. "I love it. And it's not too much. Right? I mean, do you think it's too much?"

I'm not sure if she's asking me or asking Erin, but I don't

really want to hear Erin's response. "No way," I say. "I didn't even put eyeliner on you. Your eyes look really natural, and so does the blush. It's called Au-Natural blush."

"Okay, good. My mom won't, like, freak out or anything?"

I shake my head. "Makeup isn't supposed to make you look like a clown or like a Broadway star or anything. It's supposed to enhance your natural beauty!"

"I didn't know I had natural beauty," Kristin says. "Remember, Erin, in eighth grade, when Jessy Eliv called me a linebacker? When Amanda Janoff called me brutal?"

Erin folds her arms across her chest and turns away from Kristin and me. "Yes, I remember," she grunts. "Now can we go, please?"

"Well, you look beautiful," I say to Kristin. "So have the best time tonight. And let me know how it is. And tell Cass I say hi."

"Totally. Thank you so much, Lucy." She pauses for a second as we're walking toward the front of the store. "Can I at least give you a tip? My mom told me I should ask."

"Um." I shrug. "I guess, if you insist."

Kristin looks around the store for a second and takes a little painted ceramic bowl with flowers on it off the shelf.

"Here. This will be your tip bowl." She laughs, puts ten dollars in it, and hands it to me. "Thank you so, so, so much."

"You're welcome." I smile and walk them to the door. Kristin's pretty smart—I'd never even thought of a tip bowl. "Bye, Erin."

"Bye, Lucy," she says, without expression.

Erin seems like a girl who is always expecting the worst and always scared of what's right around the corner. Kristin is the leader, and Erin just follows along. But Erin's freaked out now—like she doesn't want her friend to change at all.

I wish Erin could just realize that it's okay, that a little makeup isn't really gonna change her best friend. Maybe it'll change her a little, make her more self-confident and even a little happier. But it's not like Kristin will morph into some kind of monster. Erin would be happier if she knew that.

Beauty tip: A face mask before a big day can
help your skin look its best.

I've been sensing Sunny's nervousness about Evan
Mass and Earth Club all morning. She's not herself. Ever since
the mall incident, she's all out of whack, like she forgot what
life used to be like before her Evan Mass crush.

She's squirmy in her seat in every class, taking her hair
out of its ponytail and pulling it back up a billion times. Even
now, I just asked her a question and she hasn't responded. I
shouldn't have to ask it three times, or tap her or shake her.
But she's on another planet.

Unfortunately for her, Earth Club is after school, so she
has to wait. I guess that's unfortunate for me too. I feel like this
crush is a monster that has eaten my friend, and I'm waiting
for the monster to spit her back up. Gross, but true.

"Sunny!" I'm trying to get her attention for the fourth
time. We're on our way to lunch, after Spanish.

Finally, she responds. "Yeah?" she says it so softly I can barely hear her.

"Do you want to trade lunches?"

"Yeah, sure." She readjusts her backpack on her shoulders. "Actually, you can just have mine. I'm not hungry."

I give her a "come on!" look. "Sunny, you have to eat."

We agree to trade, which is lucky for me, and unlucky for her. Grandma made me a boring turkey sandwich with honey mustard, but I saw Sunny's lunch earlier this morning when we were at our lockers. It's leftover mushroom pizza. Cold. My favorite.

It was probably wrong to get Sunny to trade lunches when she's so vulnerable and out of it. But I don't get the chance to have cold pizza that often.

We make our way to the lunch table, and it feels like I'm guiding Sunny, like she's wearing a blindfold. Her head looks wobbly, and she's staring at what seems like nothing. I know this look; I remember when Claudia went through this, when she was in love with Barry Lyman. It wasn't fun then, and it's definitely not fun now.

When we're sitting, Sunny hands me her lunch bag, and I hand her mine. She inspects the lunch, not overly pleased but not annoyed either. "Oh, Kettle Chips, my fave," she says, not sounding at all like they really are her *fave*.

・・・

When we get to Earth Club, I plop myself right down next to Evan so that Sunny's close to him.

"Lucy, are you going to Marnie Kastman's bat mitzvah?" Evan asks me. I guess he doesn't even want to talk to Sunny anymore since she acted so weird at the mall.

"Um, no," I say hesitantly, debating what to say next. "I wasn't invited."

"Oh," Evan says, and Sunny kicks me in the shin.

When Evan turns away to talk to Brent, Sunny whispers, "See, we're not cool enough for him. I told you."

"Shh!" I say, kicking her back. "Who cares about Marnie Kastman?"

Marnie Kastman and Erica Crane are like a dynamic duo of obnoxiousness. I wouldn't want to go to her bat mitzvah even if I were invited. I don't know why Sunny cares.

"Okay, quiet down, quiet down," Mrs. Deleccio says. "We're going to continue our research today, but I also need the group of people who were interested in doing the anti-Styrofoam campaign to start working on that."

I whisper to Sunny, "I'm doing the research." She should know that by now, but lately it's hard to tell what she knows and doesn't know, and I wanted to make it clear.

"Me too," she says.

"Me three," Evan whispers, laughing.

Yamir and most of the other eighth graders go to the front of the room to go over the anti-Styrofoam letter-writing campaign with Mrs. Deleccio, and the rest of us go to the computers to start our research.

Sunny sits down next to me but just stares at her screen, opening up a Web site whenever Mrs. Deleccio walks by so she'll think Sunny's actually doing something.

"What's wrong with you?" I ask. "Why do you look like something horrible just happened?"

She makes a face at me like I should know the answer to that.

"You're still upset about Marnie Kastman?"

She nods.

"Get over it, Sunny," I say. "C'mon, we have research to do."

I'm a little surprised that I'm eager to go back to researching. I mean, I'm tired from school and I'd rather be at home on the couch, or at least in the Relaxation Room, but the research was fun last time. It was inspiring to see what average, run-of-the-mill people can do to help the world.

We hear about celebrities doing important stuff all the time: Oprah, Ellen, Angelina, and Bono. But from this research, I've realized that even a twelve-year-old from Connecticut can do stuff. Even if it's only making sure to turn off the light when I leave a room.

"Sunny, look, this school has a solar-powered water fountain," I say, trying to get her involved. "We can click this link to find the companies that make them."

"Wow," she says, as unenthusiastically as possible. She puts her head down on her desk. "I hate this club. It's like a billion hours of extra homework."

I can't even believe this. She's the reason I'm here, and now I care more about this stuff than she does.

I don't really admit this to people usually, but I like research. It's like a hobby to me in a way. It started when I had to write a report on Connecticut history in fifth grade and Claudia helped me do all this online research. I loved finding all these random tidbits from different Web sites. It was fun, like finding secret facts or buried artifacts.

Next year, in eighth grade, we have a whole class dedicated to research. I definitely don't tell people this, but I'm actually excited for it.

At the end of Earth Club, we all regroup, and Mrs. Deleccio hands each of us a bag of Hershey's Kisses. "I just wanted to say that I am so proud of all of you for all your hard work," she says.

"I'll meet you outside in a sec," I tell Sunny. "I just have to ask Mrs. Deleccio something."

Sunny makes a face at me like she thinks I'm up to something. That's one of the problems with doing everything with your best friend—if you ever need a minute to do something alone, your friend gets paranoid.

"Mrs. Deleccio, may I ask you something?" I say. I'm very careful with my *mays* and *cans* now.

"Sure, Lucy. What is it?" Mrs. Deleccio sits down at her desk and unwraps a Hershey's Kiss. Yamir told me she has a secret stash of chocolate in her supply cabinet.

"Well, one day at Earth Club when we were researching, I found this grant online that Mayor Danes is offering, like for local businesses to go green," I start. "And, um, I think it could be really good for my family's pharmacy. Will you look it over when I'm done? Before I send it in?"

Mrs. Deleccio smiles at me in that way teachers do when they're really proud of a student. "That's great that you found that, Lucy! I am so proud of you!"

"Thanks." I smile.

"But I think you should talk to your mom first and see if it's something she'd like to do. It involves a lot of paperwork." She pauses and smiles again. "You know, grown-up stuff."

I hate when people, especially teachers, talk to kids that

way. I really hate it. Actually, it makes me so angry that I get even more determined. Now I am definitely going to fill out that grant application right away. No more putting it off.

I'll show her.

"Thanks," I say, forcing myself to be nice. "See you tomorrow."

21

Beauty tip: Don't pick at your face when you're nervous or anxious.

𝒯*he next day,* I text Claudia. After spending three hours reading over the grant application, highlighting and looking up words in the dictionary, I realize that Mrs. Deleccio may be right, just a little bit. I do need help. But at least I'm grown-up enough to admit it. And it's not *so* hard that I need Mom or Grandma. Claudia will know what to do.

Claud. WHERE ARE U? Call me ASAP.

An hour later, she still hasn't responded, so I text her again. I called her as soon as I got home last night to tell her, but of course she didn't call me back.

Claauuuuudddddddiiiiiaaaaa. Calllll meeeeeee. Pleeeeaaaaaassse.

She writes back: *Calm down, Lucy. I'll call soon.*

It's easy for her to tell me to calm down, because she doesn't know the news that I'm about to tell her. Now I wish I'd told her about the grant as soon as I found it.

As I'm waiting for her to call, I go downstairs and fill up a big glass of water. Then I decide to read the grant application over back upstairs at my desk. The more I read, the more excited I get. I can actually do this. I mean, *we* can actually do this. We can actually save the store. Mom and Grandma will be happy, and life will go back to the way it used to be.

When my cell phone rings, I don't even say hello. Instead I say, "Go to www.OldMill.gov. Click on News from Mayor Danes."

"What in the world are you talking about?" she asks. "If Mom's in jail for protesting something, please tell me."

"Ha-ha," I say, staring at the screen and hoping she'll also be looking at it in a second.

"The bicentennial celebration?" Claudia asks with a snort. "This is what you've been nagging me about?"

"No, dummy. Below that."

It takes her a few seconds, but then she says, "Mayor Danes's Going Green Grant, for local, independently owned businesses of Old Mill."

"Uh-huh!" I yell.

"I'm reading," she says.

She's quiet again for a while.

Finally she says, "Oh my God. Lucy. How did you find this?"

I tell her all about Earth Club and everything, and how I

stumbled on it a few weeks ago, but how I really want to do it now, especially after what Morrie was saying.

"You're so smart, Lucy!" she says.

"But you have to help me," I tell her. "I can't fill this out by myself."

She pauses for a second. "You didn't tell Mom and Grandma?"

"Not yet." I take a sip of water. "Grandma's not gonna get it. What does she know about going green? And Mom may be into it, but she's already overwhelmed as it is. Half the time she forgets to make my lunch! And you know how important lunch is to me!"

She laughs. "Yeah, let's not tell them yet. Let me work on it. 'Kay?"

"Okay," I say, suddenly feeling a nervous pit in my stomach.

"But I can't do it right away. I have three papers due next week." She sighs. "I gotta go. Love you."

"Love you too. But look at it. Okay? We only have until the end of the year."

All afternoon at the pharmacy, I daydream about what would happen if we got this grant. I imagine myself on the local news, with Mom and Grandma and Claudia too. And they're all saying how I saved the day.

I want to save this pharmacy. But last night as I was trying to fall asleep, I realized something else. I want to be the one who saves the day, the one who makes things better.

"Lu-Lu. Lu-Dog." A voice is coming from the front of the pharmacy. An annoying, scratchy, boy voice. Only one person in the world can sound that annoying.

Yamir Ramal.

"Lu, where are you?"

I fold my arms across my chest and walk toward the front of the store. Yamir's standing there with his buddies. His equally annoying eighth-grade friends, Clint and Anthony. I think they're his only two friends in the whole world.

"So, what can you offer us, Lu?" Yamir asks. "Can we get some kind of employee discount?"

I squint at him, pursing my lips together. He has got to be kidding. "Um, no. And for your information, times are tough for Old Mill Pharmacy. And for more of your information, I wouldn't give you a discount anyway."

"Lu," Yamir says again and puts a hand on my shoulder. "No reason to get so upset. No reason at all." Then he breaks out laughing, and so do Clint and Anthony. They raid the snack aisle, and when they're done they each have at least three bags of candy—the big, jumbo-size bags.

"We want sodas from the fountain," Clint says. "Like the good old days."

Clint remembers the good old days? I doubt it. Plus, Grandma's really the only one who ever serves sodas. And I'm sure she's having one of her daily fights with my mother right now. But I'm glad they ask—maybe my idea of the pharmacy becoming a hangout is slowly coming to pass.

"Yeah, serve up some soda," Anthony says.

"Ever heard of saying please?" I smirk at them. But then I add, "I'll go see what I can do."

The boys sit down on the counter stools and I walk away. I gently put my ear up to the office door. Surprisingly, I don't hear any yelling. I knock.

"Come in!" Mom sings.

When I open the door, Grandma's sitting at the computer, and Mom is organizing the office shelves. "*Sweet Caroline. Ba ba ba,*" they sing at the same time. They then burst out laughing.

Grandma and Mom are singing? And not fighting? What a weird day at Old Mill Pharmacy.

"Grandma, some boys want sodas," I say.

"Okay. The smaller bottles are a dollar fifty, the bigger ones are two twenty-five."

"No, they want fountain sodas. It's Sunny's brother and a few of his friends."

Grandma looks up from the computer; there's a tiny sparkle in her eye. I know she's happy about this.

"Oh, Luce, give them a few bags of kettle corn," Mom adds. "On the house. My treat."

"Jane," Grandma says, laughing. "Maybe you're the reason we're struggling! You're always giving stuff away!"

Mom laughs and throws up her hands.

"What can I get you boys?" Grandma asks once she's left the office and is walking over to them. She has her Old Mill Pharmacy apron on, the one that Flo embroidered for her about twenty-five years ago. It has the pharmacy's name on the front in pale pink curlicue script and her name underneath in matching print.

Yamir and his friends order the sodas and hang out for a while. I know they're just killing time before their movie starts, but that's okay. They're hanging out here, like I'd hoped, and they've spent about twenty dollars. And they actually ordered something from the counter.

Did Mrs. Ramal force them to come here? Is this some kind of pity shopping? Or maybe Yamir's not as completely awful as I thought. Whatever it is, I'm just glad to have a few customers.

22

Business tip: Try to stay on the pulse of all
that's happening in your field.

"Are you even working on the grant appli-
cation?" I ask Claudia over the phone. I don't mean to sound
rude, but I'm not sure she's taking this as seriously as she
should.

"I told you, I have a ton going on right now, Lucy." Claudia
slurps her drink. "Did you even bother to read the last section
of the application?"

"Ummm . . ." I don't have it in front of me, so I don't
really know what she's talking about. "Maybe?"

"We need to come up with a game plan for how we'd like
to enhance our store," she says. "It's more than just a Going
Green Grant. You know that, right?"

Suddenly I'm feeling nervous, like I never should have
gotten excited about this and it's all going to fall through.
"What do you mean?"

"Okay, Lucy." She pauses, like she's trying to find words that I can understand. "Mayor Danes wants local businesses to go green but also to expand so that big chain stores don't totally take over. But the thing is, I'm not sure we really want to expand. A pharmacy is a pharmacy, you know?"

"Yeah, Morrie said the same thing," I tell Claudia. "That people like to get more than one type of item at a place. But all I could think of was the health food Mom wants to start selling and the DVD rentals, like at the grocery store."

"Yeah . . . ," Claudia says. "Those are kind of lame—no offense. If we're doing this, we might as well do it. Dream big. Know what I mean?"

"Yeah," I mumble.

Claudia tells me to hold on, and she yells out to a crowd of people that there's some kind of party at a place called McSaddle's and that they're all going over there at nine.

Thinking about all of this, I realize that I've kind of expanded already without even knowing it. I mean, the Relaxation Room. The makeup. Helping Courtney Adner with her hair trauma.

Claudia gets back on the phone and says, "I gotta go in a sec, Luce. If we can't think of anything, we'll just do the health food thing. I'm sure we can always change it later, if we win." She doesn't say anything for a second. "Listen,

I just want to tell you—I think it's a long shot that we're going to win. I don't want to burst your bubble or anything, but I need to warn you."

"Connecticut needs an eco-spa," I say, out of the blue. Suddenly it seems like an idea that has been percolating in my brain for a while has finally come together. Finally I've figured out what to do with my love of makeovers! "Like the one you went to for your birthday."

"Yeah, I know. Right? How awesome would that be?" Claudia says, like she's forgotten what we were just talking about. She gets distracted very easily, especially since she's been at college.

"No, I mean that's what we'll write. That's our way to expand! That's what we need to do to save the pharmacy."

"Oh, Luce," Claudia says in her "you're cute" tone. "That's like *way* expanding. It's opening a new business altogether."

"That's what Morrie said. That we needed to really start something new. He even said his son wanted to invest!"

"Really?"

"Yeah, and when you think about it, I practically already have a spa! The Relaxation Room! I guess I was on my way to having a spa the day I solved Courtney Adner's hair crisis. And think of the makeup applications I could do!"

In the background, I hear a guy yell, "Claudia. Par-tay tiiiiiiime!" She laughs.

"Okay. That's good! I'll write that down," Claudia says to me, sounding optimistic. "Can't hurt. And if Morrie suggested it, then it really can't hurt."

After we hang up the phone, I can't stop thinking about the eco-spa. If this really happens, it will be amazing. Completely and totally amazing. All because of Earth Club and my exceptional eavesdropping skills that day Morrie was at the store.

Then, after we have the spa and it's fabulously successful, I can have my own line of makeup to sell at the spa! Maybe I'm closer to being like Laura Mercier than I realized!

23

Don't test foundation on the back of your hand. It's a simple way to see what a color looks like, but the skin there is very different from the skin on your face. Apply it right on your cheek. Remember, the perfect color should practically disappear. —Laura Mercier

Kristin may not be Miss Popular, but ever since I did her makeup, swarms of girls have been coming in and asking me about it. They tell me they don't usually wear makeup but they have their cousin's wedding and they want to look good or they have a family friend's bat mitzvah or even just a school dance.

It's mostly just the high school girls who are into it. The girls in my grade only wear lip-gloss, and the eighth-grade girls think they're too cool to have their makeup done by a seventh grader.

"Good afternoon. Old Mill Pharmacy," I say, checking quickly to make sure I took the phone off speaker. "Yes, this is

Lucy." Mom always tells me to say "This is she," but that just sounds weird, so formal and awkward. Plus, I like my name.

"Oh, sure I can," I tell the person on the other end of the line. "I can do makeup any Saturday or Sunday and any afternoon after school."

The woman on the other end of the line tells me she wants me to do her daughter's makeup for her sweet sixteen. She heard about me from her next-door neighbor.

"So we'd need your first appointment of the day on Saturday. Saturday, June twelfth," the woman says.

I gulp. "June twelfth? But it's only November."

"How old are you?" she asks me, suddenly sounding suspicious. Hmmm. Maybe her next-door neighbor didn't tell her the full story. I'm tempted to lie, because this could be really good for business. However, she will find out the truth eventually.

"I'm twelve," I say. "But trust me, I know what I'm doing."

"Ummm-hmmmm," she says. "Okay, mark us down for that day. My name is Amy Romero."

"Got it," I say. "Well, see you then, or hopefully before!"

After I hang up with Amy, I realize that I may not be able to keep my little business a secret from Mom and Grandma much longer. Customers are actually calling me in advance, and I'm writing the appointments down on the last page of my planner for school. I need an actual appointment book and an answering service to take calls for me when I'm in school.

A few days later, I'm doing Lillian Bertella's makeup for her Quinceañera. We're in the Relaxation Room, where I've done all of my makeup jobs before. It goes fine, but after I'm done, Mom comes up to me.

"What were you doing in there?" Mom asks.

I look back at the Relaxation Room as if I don't know what she's talking about. I wonder if I should lie. But before I have the chance to decide, words start pouring out of my mouth: "I was doing someone's makeup."

"What?"

I swallow hard. "Like, you know, like people do it at Saks. Or at a spa." I clench my teeth. My mom looks horrified, and I'm not sure what to do.

"Yeaahh . . ." Mom drags out the word. "For what purpose?"

"Because it's her Quinceañera. And she wanted to look good. That's how Laura Mercier got started," I say. "And it's bringing customers into the store. After I do the girls' makeup, they buy the products!"

"And why didn't you tell anyone about this?" Mom asks.

"I told Claudia." I shrug. "She thought it was awesome. Plus, I've been doing this for a while now. I kinda thought you knew about it."

Mom shakes her head at that, like I'm completely crazy. She and Grandma must have been really distracted to never have noticed me doing it.

"What's going on here?" Grandma asks, walking over to us. "Jane, I need you in the back. You've been dillydallying all day."

"Lucy's been doing makeup for people," Mom says, her arms folded across her chest.

"Good for you, Luce. I'm glad to see you're keeping busy while you're here. And I'm sure the customers all think it's very cute." She looks at Mom and smiles in this "oh, isn't our Lucy dear" kind of way.

"Cute? No. People actually make appointments with me. A mom just called about her daughter's sweet sixteen in June!" Now I'm mad. It would have been one thing if they were angry with me. But for them to just think this is some kind of joke? No way. If they can't even take this seriously, how will they take it when I tell them about the grant and the eco-spa we're going to open?

"Really?" Grandma seems a little more interested now.

I nod. "I've been doing this for a while. It's kind of weird you guys haven't noticed," I say, out loud this time. Mom and Grandma look at each other and shrug. "And I'm also surprised you haven't noticed how much more makeup we've been selling since I started doing this. It's bringing in a ton of business!"

Grandma smiles "Lucy, what an entrepreneur you're becoming."

"Thanks, Grams." I smile and start walking toward the back office. "'Kay, I gotta go finish my vocab homework."

As I'm walking away, I hear Mom and Grandma talking, still standing by the Relaxation Room.

"She really thinks she's going to save this pharmacy, doesn't she?" Grandma asks. "I like to see that kind of drive. But I hate to say, I don't think she can do it."

"Ma. Can we have one day without your 'the world is ending' speech? Please."

"Jane, I'll stop with that when you face reality."

"Why do you want to crush Lucy? Huh? Make her feel like she can't work toward anything?"

"Forget it, Janie." Grandma says this under her breath, but I can still hear her. "Just forget it."

Maybe my mom thinks Grandma's pessimistic attitude is crushing my dreams, but it's not. I know Grandma's faith is just running out.

That's why I need to pick up where she left off. When they find out about the grant and the spa, they'll see how much I can do, how much I can help. Then they'll realize that I can save the pharmacy.

I can't wait to tell them. And I can't wait for the day when adults take kids seriously.

24

Business tip: Make sure to take a personal day
when you've reached your limit.

The next few days are completely grant-
filled. Claudia's papers are finally done, and we're texting,
e-mailing, calling, pretty much using every known form of
communication to discuss the grant. She's read over all the
rules and regulations, and now she's going to start going
through it section by section, keeping me posted on her
progress. She's staying at school for Thanksgiving, so she
has lots of time.

And it seems like right after Grandma says I won't be able
to save the pharmacy, the store gets busier and busier. It's like
in elementary school, when we used to have Opposite Day.
Like everything is the opposite of what Grandma said.

I don't want to take too much of the credit, but
the Relaxation Room is where everyone waits for their
prescriptions. Before the Relaxation Room, customers would

come in, drop them off, and then come back later. Or they'd even pay extra for delivery, before we let Tory go.

But now they sometimes stay and wait. They hand Mom or Grandma their prescription slip, and then they come to the Relaxation Room and either read a magazine or close their eyes for a minute. They buy a drink or a snack. Sometimes they make phone calls, and even though at first I was going to post a sign that said NO CELL PHONES, now I think it's okay. They usually talk pretty quietly anyway.

Mrs. Ramal will be here in ten minutes to pick me up, but a part of me doesn't want to go to Sunny's to hang out. Right now there are four people in the Relaxation Room. They're chatting with one another. Two of them bought magazines, and one, a teacher, bought a whole box of chocolates to hand out to her first-grade class tomorrow.

"Sunny, you're never going to believe this," I say once Mrs. Ramal arrives and I'm in the car. "Mrs. Ramal, you won't believe it either."

"What?" Mrs. Ramal turns down the Indian music she has playing. She always listens to Indian music. I've heard these songs so many times, I practically know all of them by heart, and sometimes I'll even join in when Sunny and her mom start singing along. I used to ask them what the songs mean, but Mrs. Ramal would just say, "Oh, these two are in love, but they live so far from one another," and then she'd go into a whole long story about it. It's better to imagine a story of my own.

"The Relaxation Room that I created is a huge hit," I say. "Just now there were four people sitting in there!"

"Wonderful, Lucy. Just wonderful," Mrs. Ramal says, smiling at me from the front seat. "When I was there the other day getting Yamir his athletic-foot cream, there were people in there. Perhaps about five, even."

Sunny laughs. "Mom, it's *athlete's foot.* Not *athletic foot.*"

I try not to laugh, but I can't help it. Mrs. Ramal's English is just a little bit off, so it's funny. She moved here from India when she was seventeen.

Mrs. Ramal shakes her head. "*Athlete's. Athletic.* I don't see a difference."

"Never mind, Mom," Sunny groans, turning to face me. "Lucy, that's so awesome!"

"I'm just happy customers are actually in the store."

Mrs. Ramal looks at me through the rearview mirror again. "Lucy, I heard about you and your makeup design. My neighbor was raving about you. She wants to come in with her daughters before her cousin's wedding."

"Oh, thanks." Wow. I can't believe how fast word is spreading.

When we get to Sunny's house, we have our favorite snack,

sugar cookies and apple cider, and then start our magazine reading. I've brought over as many old ones from the pharmacy as I could find. We kick off our sneakers, spread out on her daybed, and dig in, folding down pages that we want to discuss with each other later on.

When I get cozy and comfortable with one of Sunny's throw pillows behind my back, Yamir barges in. He's carrying their pug, Oscar, in his arms and blowing bubbles with bright red gum.

"Yamir!" Sunny shrieks. "Get out of here!"

Ignoring her, he plops himself down on Sunny's beanbag chair. Oscar hops out of his arms and onto Sunny's bed, crumpling up the magazines as he walks over them.

"I mean it, get out!" Sunny yells again.

"Calm down, Sunner," he says. "I came to talk to Lucy. Not you."

"Huh?" I say.

"I heard you're a makeup artist." Yamir clears his throat. "Will you do my makeup for the eighth-grade masquerade?"

"Yamir, what planet are you from?" Sunny asks.

"What? It's totally normal. The eighth graders do it every year. I mean, they've never gotten their makeup done professionally before, but they do wear makeup every year." Yamir grins. "I can bring Lucy tons of business."

Sunny gives me a "what on earth is he talking about?" look, but part of me is flattered. And it is a whole new market that I'd never even thought of before.

"Thanks, Yamir," I say. "Let's talk about this when it gets closer to the dance."

He scoops Oscar off Sunny's bed. "Gets closer? It's in, like, two weeks, right before the winter vacation. Get with the program, Lu." He lowers his head and squints at me. "Later, losers."

"I had no idea the eighth-grade masquerade was so soon," I say to Sunny. "Did you?"

Sunny doesn't answer. She's still giving me that "Yamir's crazy" look long after he's left the room. I can tell she wants me to say something about how annoying he is, but I don't feel like it. He is annoying, but he wants to help the business. I can't argue with that.

"Knock, knock," Mrs. Ramal says before knocking on Sunny's door.

"Come in," Sunny says.

"Lucy, are you staying for dinner?" Mrs. Ramal asks.

I smile. "Oh, no, I can't tonight. Mom, Grandma, and I are going out for pizza."

"That's right." Mrs. Ramal smiles like she knew that but wanted an excuse to come in here. "Okay, well don't leave yet. Giri will be home in a minute, and he has something to tell you."

Sunny looks confused. "Dad has something to tell Lucy?"

Mrs. Ramal smiles and closes the door.

"What could my dad have to tell you?" Sunny asks.

"I have no idea." I shrug. Sunny sometimes gets all weird about dads. I think it's because she feels like I'll get upset or something since I barely even see my own dad. It's a little way that Sunny looks out for me. But dads don't bother me. Besides, Sunny's dad is really nice.

"Room service!" Sunny's dad yells through the door, trying to be funny.

"Dad, what do you want?" Sunny yells back. He opens the door. Mrs. Ramal is standing next to him. I wonder what they're about to tell us. One second I think it's something serious. But with Sunny's dad's joking, it can't be that serious.

"Lucy, as you know, we're remodeling the downstairs," Mrs. Ramal says. "And thankfully, Giri has allowed me to decorate this time, since he did such a pitiful job last time."

"She will never let me forget it," Sunny's dad says. "My wife is forcing me to get rid of the Turbo Massage Chair 7000. I have no choice. She will either get rid of the chair or get rid of me. And I couldn't live without her." He looks at Mrs. Ramal and gives her a kiss on the forehead. "So, Lucy. I want you to have the Turbo Massage Chair 7000. It is a wonderful chair, and I have only used it about three and a half times. It turns out I prefer regular chairs."

We all laugh. I'm not really sure why Mr. Ramal wants me, of all people, to have the chair, but it's kind of cool. "Oh, um, thank you, Mr. Ramal."

"For your Relax Room," he says, and then looks at Mrs. Ramal and Sunny.

"Relaxation Room, Dad," Sunny says. "But close enough."

Mr. Ramal nods. "Right. So what could be better for a Relaxation Room than the Turbo Massage Chair 7000?"

Finally, it's sinking in. This is so, so, so fabulous! "Oh my God. Thank you so much! Thank you so, so, so much!" I hop up from Sunny's bed and give Mr. Ramal the biggest hug I've ever given him in the seven years that I've known him.

I look back at Sunny to see if she knew about this, but she looks as surprised as I am. I wonder when they decided about this.

"You're very welcome," Mr. Ramal says.

The pizza place where Mom, Grandma, and I are going for dinner is around the corner from Sunny's house, so I call Mom on her cell phone to tell her that I'll walk and meet them there. I decide to tell them the good news about the chair in person.

As I'm walking over, gratitude washes over me. I'm so lucky. I'm one of the luckiest twelve-year-olds in the world, I bet. I have Sunny for a best friend, and Sunny comes with the awesomest parents in the universe. And I can do makeup. People actually want me to do makeup.

I know things are getting better. I just know it. And I haven't even told Mom and Grandma about the grant and spa yet. That is going to be amazing. Maybe I'll even see if I can borrow the Ramals' video camera so that I can record it when I tell them.

25

The right makeup can really emphasize your eye color.
—*Laura Mercier*

*W*e're not allowed to use cell phones in school, and I try to follow that rule. But right now, I just can't. So much is going on with the grant, and I'm at school for Earth Club until at least five thirty. I need to check in with Claudia.

Wut is happening wit grant?

Friend Bean is looking it over with me.

Bean?

Nickname. Talk later. ILY

"Ready, Luce?" Sunny comes up behind me and puts her arm around me.

"Yup," I say. "Claudia has a friend named Bean. Weird, huh?"

"Really weird."

"So are you ready to actually talk to Evan today?" I ask

Sunny. "'Cuz I'm running out of patience. I'm in this Earth Club for you, y'know."

Sunny rolls her eyes. They look extra green today because of the pale green eye shadow I gave her and smudged on her eyelids after Social Studies. "Hello! Remember the grant? The one that will probably save your business? You wouldn't know about it without Earth Club."

I shake my head at her. "Maybe you're a little bit right. But let's not get crazy about it saving the business—we may not even get it."

"Confidence goes a long way, you know," she says, mocking me.

I guess we're late, because when we get to Mrs. Deleccio's classroom, everyone's already sitting down, and she's standing at the front of the room ready to start the meeting.

"Find a seat, girls, please," she says. "If our goal is to go to the first school board meeting of the year, in the fall, and present our proposal for going green, then we have a lot of work to do. We're going to split into small groups today, so there will be two to three people per computer."

"Can we pick partners?" Annabelle Wilson asks. "Please."

"Not today," Mrs. Deleccio says. "I want you all to learn about working with others, not just your friends."

Everyone says, "Awwww, man," and "No fair," and stuff

like that. I look over at Sunny, and she's biting her nails and tapping her foot at the same time. If Mrs. Deleccio assigns Evan and Sunny to work together, Sunny may pass out right here. That really won't be good.

"Okay, raise your hands if you want to do the fields cleanup," Mrs. Deleccio says. All the sixth-grade boys raise their hands for that, and so do a few eighth-grade girls. Mrs. Deleccio sends all of them to the right side of the classroom. "Now raise your hands if you want to do the research on going green in school. But I need serious commitments now. I know some of you have been doing this all along, but now we're really getting into the nitty-gritty."

Sunny and Evan and I and a few of his friends, Yamir and a few of his friends, Annabelle, and a few others raise our hands for this one. Sunny, Annabelle, and I end up working together. It's not as good as a Sunny and Evan pairing, but I'm glad Sunny and I get to stick together.

"Wait! Sorry I'm late!" We all turn around and see Erica Crane running in, her imitation Louis Vuitton bag hanging off her wrist. "Sorry, Mrs. Deleccio. I had another after-school commitment."

Yeah, right. That girl is trouble with a capital *T.* Why is she even here? She was never in Earth Club before.

"Take a seat, Erica," Mrs. Deleccio says. She explains who

is doing what, and Erica walks right over to our side of the room. But she doesn't do what I expect her to—she doesn't sit next to me so she can bug me the entire time. Instead, she sits next to Yamir. Then she flips her hair over her shoulder; some of it even lands on the computer keyboard. "Hey, Yami," she says, all flirty.

Yami?

Sunny and I look at each other at the exact same second.

Erica Crane flirting with Yamir? No way. No way. No way!

Then Clint says, "Hey, Yami," imitating Erica. And Anthony says, "What's up, Yami? Yami Pajami?"

"Guys, shut up, okay?" Yamir says. And I'm not sure whose cheeks turn the reddest: Yamir's, Sunny's, or mine.

Erica's, on the other hand, stay perfectly white and freckled.

It takes all the effort I can muster to focus on the going-green research. I don't know why this Erica Crane thing is weirding me out so much. Why do I even care? It's just Yamir.

Even though I liked it better when we could research on our own, working as a group isn't so bad. When it's my turn at the computer, I find the most amazing Web site. Annabelle and Sunny pull their chairs in closer.

"Do you guys see this?" I ask. "It's all these ways the cafeteria can be more earth friendly. They could change the kinds of paper products they use, get recycled-plastic utensils, and even buy recycled-plastic lunch trays."

"Yeah. I hadn't even thought of the cafeteria," Annabelle says. "Probably because I always bring my lunch!"

"I'm printing this page out," I say, already clicking to the next section of the site, which talks about heating and cooling systems in schools.

"Make sure you're documenting all your sources," Mrs. Deleccio calls out from the front of the classroom. "If we are going to the school board, we need to have a very professional demonstration."

"This lightbulb thing is really easy to do," Sunny says, reading over my shoulder. "Look, it says it's even cheaper to order in bulk. We could make sure the head of facilities or whoever stocks up."

"Good idea," Annabelle says.

"Sunny, what'd you just say about the lightbulbs?" Evan asks from a few computer stations away.

"Um, uh, just that the school should stock up, and it's cheaper that way," Sunny mumbles, fiddling with the strands of hair hanging outside her ponytail.

"That's an awesome idea," Evan says. I discreetly kick

the side of my shoe against the side of Sunny's. She kicks me back.

Mrs. Deleccio tells us that it's time to wrap up. Before I turn off the computer, I quickly e-mail myself all the links I found.

On our way out, I stop and talk to Mrs. Deleccio. "I found so much stuff on making the cafeteria green, so can I be in charge of that part of the proposal?"

"Yes, definitely," she says, smiling. "That's a really great idea. I'm going to write it down. You can give me and the rest of the club updates periodically, okay?"

"Sure. Oh, and Sunny's gonna help, okay?" I look at Sunny. She nods.

"Great, girls. Have a good night!"

On her way out of the classroom, Erica says, "Bye, Yami."

Sunny and I shake our heads at each other and follow Yamir to Mrs. Ramal's car.

On the way home, all I can think about is making the proposal to the school board in the fall and how I'm in charge of the cafeteria part. I'm going to have to speak in front of everyone, but I'll be in eighth grade then, and I bet I'll feel more confident. But I'll have to really know what I'm talking about. Imagine if it goes through, and it really works, and Old Mill Middle School actually becomes a green school.

Think about all the people that would affect. All the energy we'd save. The earth would be healthier just because of us.

I just can't get enough. Like, my heart beats really fast when I think about it, and sometimes I can't even fall asleep at night because there's so much to do.

26

"What's new at Earth Club?" Mom asks as she's squeezing fresh OJ for me. She thinks breakfast is the most important meal of the day, and she always makes an effort to actually make breakfast and not just give me a granola bar or a banana as I run out the door.

I love these moments when she makes my breakfast and I can sit at the table and just start the day out leisurely.

But today Mom looks worn out and exhausted and has dark circles under her eyes. I really, really want to tell her about the grant because I think it'd make her feel better. But I know it's too soon.

"Nothin' much," I say.

"What kind of stuff are you working on?" she asks.

"Recycling, letter-writing campaigns, research. That type of thing." I pick up the newspaper that's sitting on the table, hoping she'll stop asking me questions if she thinks I'm reading.

"That's great that you're doing this, Lucy," she says. "I'm really proud of you."

Sometimes I feel like my mom can read my mind.

After breakfast, we head over to the pharmacy. Today's Saturday and Mr. Ramal is coming to the pharmacy to drop off the massage chair. Sunny said she'd come with him and then she'd stay and hang out with me for the rest of the day.

When I told Mom and Grandma about the chair, they were really thrilled, but they asked all their usual questions: "Does Mr. Ramal really want to get rid of the chair?" "Why doesn't he want it anymore?" "Should we offer to pay for it?"

Of course I told them that it's a gift and that Mrs. Ramal is redecorating and all of that stuff. Mom and Grandma are such worriers. If they don't have a specific thing worrying them at that minute, they'll find something.

Sunny calls to say they're on their way, and I tell the people in the Relaxation Room that we're getting a delivery, just so that they'll be prepared. There are two little old ladies in there gossiping about this other lady who lives on their block and who just started dating a man from around the corner.

I've been eavesdropping; I'll admit it. It may seem weird,

eavesdropping on little old ladies. But they're really good storytellers.

"Giri, this is so wonderful of you," my mom says to Mr. Ramal, greeting him and Sunny at the door. "Are you sure we can't give you something?"

"Jane, don't mention it. Really. It is my pleasure to add such a small thing to your lovely store," Mr. Ramal says. I love the formal way he talks. Everything sounds so much more truthful, like he means everything he says and isn't just saying it to be nice.

"Well, thank you," Mom says, following behind as Mr. Ramal wheels in the chair. Sunny's skipping behind them, the way she used to do when we were little. She loved skipping more than anyone I'd ever known.

Sunny plops herself down on one of the couches and closes her eyes. "I'm already relaxed," she says.

"What do you have to not be relaxed about?" Mr. Ramal asks, and then smooshes Sunny's hair. "Your life is cherry pie."

"Dad." Sunny rolls her eyes at him. "I have tests. I have reports. I have—"

That's when I burst out laughing, and Sunny does too. We both know what she has to be stressed about.

Soon the chair is all moved in and set up, and Mr. Ramal

explains to Mom and me how it works. It looks great in the Relaxation Room, in the corner between the two couches. I just know that people are going to love that chair. It fits right in—like it was always supposed to be here.

"Bye, ladies," Mr. Ramal says. "Sunita, I will pick you up around five."

Sunny usually hates when anyone calls her Sunita. But from her dad, it's okay.

"Lucy, make sure to write Mr. Ramal a thank-you note for the chair," Mom says.

After that, Sunny and I take turns using the massage chair, testing out all of the different settings. Then we figure we should get up so that other people can use it.

"Let's spy on who's going to the movies," Sunny says. "I bet Evan and his friends go every Saturday. Don't you think?"

I give her a look. "I have no idea. But that would be really annoying if we spent the whole day spying and they never showed."

Sunny nods. "So, what should we do now?"

"Let's go make sure all the vitamins are in order. And then if everything looks okay, we'll go get ice cream."

Sunny follows me to the back of the store, near the prescription counter. I make sure the vitamins and diet aids are organized in alphabetical order, the way Grandma likes it. Sunny hovers over me, telling me when I've made a mistake.

"Can you believe Evan talked to me at Earth Club? He said my idea was awesome."

"Yes," I groan. Sunny's asked me this question a billion times now.

"You can believe it?" she asks again.

"Yes! You're awesome, Sunny. Hello? I've been trying to tell you that."

She smiles.

After a few seconds of silence, Sunny asks, "This is what you do all day? I mean, it's fun and all. But all day every day?"

"You know I'm not here every day." I move a bottle of vitamin B to the right shelf. "But I do other stuff too. The makeup, hair tips, y'know."

"What on earth are Loozemore gels?" Sunny asks, picking up a bottle.

"These new FDA-approved weight-loss pills, over-the-counter."

"Do they work?" Sunny asks.

"I doubt it." I shrug. "I don't think any of those things work."

"You're practically a pharmacist," Sunny says, laughing. "Where are your mom and grandma right now?"

Good question. I haven't seen them for a few minutes, and the office door is open, so I know they're not in there. I look around, and then I see them at the front of the store, talking to two girls. The girls look like they're in eighth or ninth grade.

"There they are," I tell Sunny. "C'mon, let's go see what they're doing. Stay quiet, and stay down behind the toy aisle."

Sunny looks confused, but she follows along anyway.

"Do you, like, sell any, um, like, perfume that also works as—" The girl starts laughing so hard she can't finish her sentence.

"Works as what?" Grandma asks.

"Works as, um, deodorant?"

"She has a nervous laugh," the other girl says.

Grandma nods. "I have a gift set of soaps and perfumes. It comes with deodorant. Would that help?"

"Yeah, I think so," the nervous-laugh girl asks, still laughing. She turns to her friend. "We have a friend, and she kinda has BO. And we want to tell her, but we don't want to make her feel bad."

Sunny taps me on my thigh. We're both sitting on our

knees on the hard pharmacy floor. "If I ever have BO, please just tell me."

I smile at her. "Okay."

Grandma says, "Lovies, you can give this set to her as a gift."

"This happened to me once, in college," Mom says. "With a friend of mine, Keith Sanders. I put a bar of Irish Spring on his bed. And don't worry, we laughed about it after."

"Okay, cool," one of the girls says.

"Here, take this too," Mom says, handing them a bottle of body wash and body lotion in one. "It's a great product."

"Jane! Again with the free stuff!" Grandma says, half-serious and half-laughing.

"Thanks so much," a girl says. "I don't know what it is, but you guys are so easy to talk to."

"Come back anytime. Let us know how it goes," Grandma says.

Finally, my knees can't take it anymore and I plop down on the pharmacy floor. Sunny and I sit there for a few minutes. We open up a package of Silly Putty and start putting it on each other's arms.

"Ew, look, it picked up my birthmark!" Sunny screeches.

"Ew. And arm hair," I say. I'm ready to put it on my knee when I suddenly become aware that someone's standing over us.

"Lucy?" I hear.

I look at Sunny, and Sunny looks at me. And then we both look up at the shadow above us.

Erica Crane is standing there. She's been there listening and watching us as we were discussing birthmarks and arm hair and playing with Silly Putty.

27

"*If this isn't a good time,* we can come back.
But shouldn't you be working or something? Don't you, like,
work here?" Erica asks.

"Yeah, I work here," I say flatly.

"I was just here with my mom, and my sister told me
about how you do makeup and stuff. No offense, but, Lucy,
you need to wear makeup. It's a good thing you do."

I grit my teeth before I say anything to her. "Do you want a
makeover?" I ask, standing up. "Sunny and I were just playing
with Silly Putty because we were bored, but I can help you."

"Yeah, I don't know how you spend so much time here,"
Erica says. "I would be, like, *so* bored. Anyway, my mom said I
could get whatever I want. My dad's being honored at this big
gala at the end of the month. It's really fancy, so I think I need
a little something."

"Okay, come with me." I roll my eyes as I walk in front of her. I wish I could refuse to help her, but a customer is a customer. Erica follows me to the makeup section and Sunny does too, although Sunny's still fiddling with the Silly Putty, stretching it out as far as it can go and then mushing it up into a little ball.

Once we're in the makeup section, I quickly study Erica's coloring. She's always been mean to me, so I never really bothered to look at her that closely. She's tall with brown hair the color of wet dirt. She has tiny eyes, brown too, and chubby cheeks.

"Oh, Sunny, by the way," Erica says. "Your brother is the cutest kid in school. Marnie and I decided."

"Ew," Sunny says.

"Do you think he likes me?" Erica asks. This is the most Erica's said to Sunny in her entire life.

"No clue."

"Well, I'm gonna try and get him to ask me to the eighth-grade masquerade," Erica proclaims. "Just wanted you to know. So, Lucy, show me what you can do."

Really? Erica Crane is going to get Yamir to ask her to the eighth-grade masquerade? That's disgusting. Yamir may be annoying, but he deserves someone nicer than Erica Crane.

I just want to get this done as quickly as possible so that

Erica will get out of my face. But she's still a customer. I know there are customers that Grandma doesn't like, but she still works with them. That's part of owning your own business, I guess. "I think you should wear really bright lipstick. And what color is the dress that you're wearing?"

Sunny gives me a look. She knows I never recommend bright lipstick, especially for girls our age. And I know it was sneaky of me to recommend it. But I can't help it. Erica's mean. And one night wearing ugly lipstick won't kill her.

But then Erica starts clapping her hands and twirling her hair. "Oh my God. I love this dress so much. It's from this fancy store in Manhattan, Bergdorf's, I think it's called. It's red. A real, true red dress. It was really expensive. I don't think you guys would wear a dress this expensive, but this gala is really important, so I had to get a really, really expensive dress."

If she says "expensive" one more time, I'm going to scream. "So then you should wear very, very bright red lipstick," I say as confidently as I can. "You have to. The brightest possible. I have the perfect color."

"Is red your favorite color or something?" Sunny asks Erica.

"Yeah. Hello. Don't you remember the dress I wore to fifth-grade graduation?"

Sunny and I nod, even though I don't remember it

whatsoever. "I think you should wear, like, a beige eye shadow. Something subtle. But it'll also bring out the brown in your eyes."

"Really?" Erica asks.

I nod. "You have a few different lines of makeup to choose from." I show Erica all of the different varieties, and soon her mother comes over to tell her they need to go pick her sister up at dance. Erica and her mom both seem happy with the selections, and they head over to Mom and the register to pay for them.

"Lucy, remember what you've been asking me for months now?" Sunny asks after Erica leaves.

"Huh?"

"How you've been begging to do my makeup." Sunny giggles. "Well, will you do it now?"

"Yes!" I squeal, clapping my hands. "But Sunny, it's not even makeup. You don't need makeup, like, every day or anything. Your mom would kill you and kill me if you started wearing makeup. She barely even wears makeup."

"So why did you want to do a makeover, then?"

"I can give you some skin-care tips, and some ideas for hair products," I say. "More useful stuff than just makeup. That's what I've been wanting to do all along!"

"Yeah! Tell me everything I need to know."

"Well, you know how your skin gets really dry in the winter?" I ask.

Sunny nods.

"Here, use this moisturizer. But not just in the winter—all year round." I hand her a bottle of Silky Pearl moisturizer. Sunny runs over to the front of the store and grabs one of our red shopping baskets.

"And your hair is kind of oily," I tell her when she gets back with the basket. "You should use this shampoo, and you don't need a lot of conditioner."

She nods and puts the shampoo in the basket. She's looking at me with wide eyes, like she wants me to tell her more.

When I don't say anything immediately, she asks, "What do I do when my skin breaks out? I only break out on my chin, but I hate it."

I look around the shelves for a product that won't be too harsh for Sunny's sensitive skin. "Here's this. It's a very gentle acne treatment, exfoliant, and concealer all in one."

"Really?"

"Only use it when you break out, though. You don't need it when your skin is clear."

Sunny can't stop looking at the products, reading over their descriptions, and asking me questions. She's so excited and reassured, almost like I just gave her a complete and total self-confidence makeover. It's so much fun to see her like this that I can't resist giving her one more thing.

"Here, Sunny. Use this lip-gloss. Best Thing Ever," I tell her.

"Pink Lollipop." She looks at the tube I just handed her and smiles. "Of course."

When Mr. Ramal gets to the pharmacy to pick her up, Sunny hands him the basket and then gets down on her knees and begs. "Please, Dad! Please, can I get this stuff? Please! Please! Please!"

"What is this?"

"Oh, it's just shampoo and skin-care stuff, Mr. Ramal," I reassure him. "Sunny was running low. I noticed when I slept over last."

Mr. Ramal smiles at me and then looks at Sunny still on her knees on the floor. "How can I say no? And not support Old Mill Pharmacy?" He looks down at Sunny again. "Sunita, get up. You've gone too far now."

Sunny gets up and brushes herself off. When her dad is paying for all of the products, she stands up on her tiptoes and whispers to me, "I can't wait to come to school on Monday after I've used my new beauty regimen."

I smile. This is what makeup is all about. It's really irrelevant if you wear a bright green eye shadow or just a pale pink; it's the way it makes you feel, the way you carry yourself when your eyelids are that color. It felt good when I helped Kristin and the other girls, but helping Sunny feels amazing.

I'm gonna be just like Laura Mercier one day. I'm gonna start my own makeup and skin-care line. I'll call it S.C. Skin Care.

Self-confidence Skin Care.

Or maybe even N.G. Skin Care. Nice Girl Skin Care.

That could do wonders for girls like Erica Crane.

Business tip: Always answer your business calls
with a cheerful, enthusiastic voice.

I know I've done a lot already to make
improvements at the store, but I feel like I still need to do
more. Claudia and I are working on the finishing touches for
the grant, and that's great and everything. But every time I see
Grandma stressed and upset, I want to find a more immediate
way to help the pharmacy. The makeup stuff was a good idea,
but now it's almost Christmas break, and people are so busy
holiday shopping that they're not really getting their makeup
done.

The only big thing I have coming up is the eighth-grade
masquerade. People say they're gonna come to me for makeup,
but who knows if they will. Eighth graders are kind of flaky.

Grandma and Flo are still on the phone all the time about
putting the house on the market, and the only reason they
haven't yet is that Flo says holiday time is the worst time to
sell a house. Everyone's busy with shopping and cooking and

planning and family togetherness, and no one's thinking about moving.

I'm happy about that. At least we have a little more time to see if things get better, and I have time to keep trying to improve things.

I'm also happy that it's almost the holidays and I get a break from school, but I'm disappointed Claudia's not coming home this year. She's going to El Salvador with a group from school to rebuild homes. That's my sister—Miss Do-Gooder. I hate to sound selfish, but I wish she were going to be here with me.

Today's the last Earth Club meeting before winter break, so I want to get a lot done. We have school next week, but all clubs are canceled so people can study for midterms and the eighth graders can prepare for the masquerade.

"Luce, look, this school has complete solar heating," Sunny tells me, pointing to the screen. I inch closer so I can read about it.

"Yeah, but that school is in Southern California. I don't think we can do that here."

"Oh yeah!" She laughs, and I laugh too, and out of the corner of my eye I see Mrs. Deleccio giving us a look.

As much as I want to get a lot done today, I can't concentrate. This always happens to me before winter break.

It feels like everything's exciting and happy and bubbly around me, and I can't help feeling that way too.

"I need a few volunteers to go collect the recycling from the boxes in the classrooms," Mrs. Deleccio says, and Evan immediately raises his hand.

I'm barely paying attention, still reading up on the solar-heated school, when I hear Sunny say, "I'll go too." My head jerks up, and I smile at her. She shrugs and whispers to me, "I can't pass up this opportunity. Look how good my hair looks from that shampoo you gave me."

I smile. "I know! Have fun!"

Sunny and Evan don't end up going alone, though, because of course Brent needs to go with Evan. I swear they're attached at the hip. But I'm not one to talk. Look at Sunny and me!

I spend the rest of the time researching eco-friendly cafeteria stuff and looking up all the different kinds of businesses that have gone green. So far, I haven't found one green pharmacy anywhere, and I haven't found any green spas in Connecticut.

"Yami," I hear Erica whisper. She's sitting next to Yamir; her chair is as close to his as possible. That girl is a little bug that seems to come out of nowhere and then won't stop crawling all over you and biting you.

"Yeah?" Yamir replies. He's typing up his description sheet

for the global-warming earth model he made a few months ago. He's convinced he's getting into the semifinals for the county science fair, and he's probably right. He made it past the first round already.

"Do you and Clint wanna go to the movies with Marnie and me this weekend?"

"Only if we can go to the Ocean Street Theater," he says, not turning to look at Erica, still staring at the screen.

"Why? They only have three screens," she complains. And when she catches me looking at her, she makes a gross face.

"It's the only theater I support. Plus, we can buy snacks at Old Mill Pharmacy before." Yamir looks up from the screen and smiles at me. But I pretend not to notice.

"Whatever," Erica says. "You're a little bizarre. But I like you anyway."

I'm the last one to leave Earth Club; Mom's picking Sunny and me up, and I know she'll be late. Plus, the more I read about all of these little things that are saving the earth, the more obsessed I get.

Take bottled water. It's so ridiculous. Some people bring a bottle of water to school every single day and then just throw the bottle out when the water's gone. That's such a huge waste. All of those bottles are sitting in some landfill somewhere.

We all feel like we're just one person, so what does it matter if we accidentally litter? Or if we throw away a glass tomato-sauce jar instead of recycling it? But it does matter. Every little bit helps, like Grandma always says.

And it's the same with the store. Every customer helps. Every little improvement helps. I feel like Earth Club has helped me realize that I can make a difference. In the world, but also in the pharmacy.

"How was recycling with Evan?" I ask Sunny in a singsong voice on the way to the parking lot.

"Well, great, except someone recycled a bottle of orange soda, and it wasn't empty, and now I have sticky old soda dripping all the way down my arm." She holds her arm out to show me.

"Ew. Gross. But how was Evan?"

She smiles. "Cute. Really cute."

Seems to me she'll be able to handle a little orange soda on her arm.

Later that night Claudia texts me: *Need to help me with a paragraph on the grant app. Almost done. Check ur email.*

I run upstairs to check my e-mail.

She needs my help on the paragraph about the strengths of the business. It says to be specific, talk about aspects that make your business unique. "You're there so much more than I am now, so you should fill this out. Don't worry, I'll proofread it after," she writes.

I have to say that it feels pretty awesome that Claudia wants me to write this section. It's true that I am at the store more than she is these days, but she could certainly write it too.

It takes me a few minutes to collect my thoughts, but once I start writing, the words flow really easily.

Old Mill Pharmacy is really more than just a pharmacy. It's a place where people come to buy candy before the movies. Where kids come to ask my grandma for advice. And just this year, it became a place where girls come for makeup tips and to get their makeup done before a special event. And it's also a place where people come to relax. We have a Relaxation Room just for that purpose. We can do more to be green, but in all of these little ways, Old Mill Pharmacy is already partly green. We have special makeup that's not tested on animals, and the Relaxation Room only uses natural light and special energy-saving lightbulbs. And people are happy when they come to Old Mill Pharmacy. Being happy is definitely an important part of going green. Because when people are happy they want to do more to help the earth. Happy people = green earth, I think.

29

Give color a chance from time to time.
It's a great mood enhancer. —*Laura Mercier*

"So, what's new, my love?" Grandma asks me.
She's sitting on the front porch in her favorite wicker rocking
chair reading the Sunday paper. She has a heat lamp next to
her to keep warm.

Sunday is her favorite day, because the pharmacy opens at
noon and closes at five. She says Sunday is the only day she has
a drop of time to herself.

"Nothing, really," I say, pulling my sweatshirt hood up.

"Nothing, really?" Grandma asks, like she knows that's
impossible.

"Well, okay. You know how I've been going to Earth
Club?"

Grandma nods.

"Well, I think we should go green. At the pharmacy."

Grandma tilts her head and smiles at me. "Lucy, you're

so sweet," she says. "I love how much you care about everything that's going on with the store."

"No, Grandma," I say. "I mean it. We can do it."

"Lucy, you're twelve. Try to stop worrying about this. Just enjoy being a kid, okay?"

"Never mind," I mumble and get up from the porch. I should have known she wouldn't take me seriously. All adults are the same that way: Grandma, Mrs. Deleccio, even my mom, most of the time. They don't think kids can do anything except go to school and have fun.

I go inside to see if Claudia has e-mailed me the grant application yet. Earlier she had said it was almost all filled out but she wanted to double-check it before we talked to Mom and Grandma about it.

I'm so excited that I'm practically skipping down the hall into the computer room. I turn on the computer, but as soon as I sign on, the computer shuts off again. So do all the lights in the house.

I figure it's a little rainstorm or something. That kind of thing happens all the time in an old town like Old Mill. But I look out the window and it's still a beautiful, sunny day.

Did a power line fall? Is something wrong with the electric company?

"Jane!" I hear Grandma calling. "Jane Scarlett Desberg. Where are you?"

Uh-oh. Suddenly I realize this has very little to do with the outside world and everything to do with my mother.

I lean my head over the railing so that I can hear their conversation downstairs.

"Ma, I paid."

"When was the last time you paid? In full." Grandma's talking in her serious voice now.

"I don't pay in full. I pay what I can pay. I've arranged a deal."

"What kind of deal?"

"A payment plan. I explained our hardship."

"Jane! What did you pay last month? I want to know figures. Amounts. Stop being so vague!"

"I didn't pay last month, Ma. I paid other bills last month."

"And the month before?"

"The electric bill was at the bottom of the pile. It might not have gotten paid."

"Jane!" Grandma's voice gets louder. "When I put you in charge of the bills I thought you could handle it. But you can't. Lucy could handle it better than you!"

Oh no. I couldn't. Really, I couldn't.

"Ma, please stop screaming."

"You have left us without electricity in the middle of winter!"

"Actually, no," Mom starts. "Winter doesn't even technically begin until December twenty-first."

I cover my mouth, trying as hard as I can not to laugh. Mom's not even trying to be funny. She's just a little bit clueless sometimes.

"You're done with the bills. All I ask is that you show up at the pharmacy and do your work."

"You think I choose not to pay the bills? That's what you think?"

Grandma doesn't respond.

"No. Not at all," Mom continues. "After I pay the pharmacy bills and the mortgage, there's very little left. Then I have to pay Claudia's tuition and go grocery shopping and buy whatever else we need. Then, with whatever tiny bit of money is left, I try to tackle the household bills."

"That's it," Grandma says. I'm tired of standing up and leaning over the railing, so I sit down on the carpet in the hallway and lean against the wall. "The pharmacy isn't succeeding at all. It's a bust at this point. This happens all the time. Local businesses closing."

"Ma, no. That's not the answer."

"What's the answer, then? Tell me."

"I don't know, but we have to try. We can't let a big company in to take our place. Do you know how they treat their employees?"

Now would be a perfect time to jump in and tell them everything, but I'm too scared. I don't want to say it at the wrong time and have them get angry and then tell me I can't apply for the grant anymore. The annoying part about being a kid is that adults can tell you what to do, and I can't stand the idea of having to give up.

Grandma doesn't say anything, but I don't need to be down there to know what's happening. I bet Grandma's making faces at my mother. Looking at her like she's lost her mind.

"We can take out a loan. A very low-interest loan."

"You're serious right now?" Grandma asks.

"One hundred percent serious."

"You're talking about getting into more debt! When we don't even have enough money to pay the electric bill?" Grandma's yelling at the top of her lungs at this point, and I'm pretty sure Mr. Bicks, next door on one side, and Mr. and Mrs. Louie, on the other side, can hear them.

"Just think about it. Because I don't see you coming up with any solutions."

After that, no one says anything. I keep thinking I need to

go and read over the grant application one more time, because now is the time to tell them. The fight clinched it. Now is the time to make them realize that there is a solution.

Luckily, there's still some battery left on my cell phone. I text Claudia: *We have to tell them. NOW.*

She texts back: *OK. I'm done with it. It's perfect. Call me when ur eating dinner and we'll tell them together.*

I don't want to tell her we don't have electricity right now. I'm just hoping it'll be back on by then.

30

Beauty tip: Crying can make your skin look blotchy and red, but it usually does make you feel better.

"*I have an announcement* to make," I tell Mom and Grandma as soon as we're sitting down to dinner. It's already almost nine, but the electricity only came back on twenty minutes ago, after Grandma begged someone over my cell phone. "And Claudia is on speaker."

"Hey, Claud," Mom says, sounding exhausted. "What a nice surprise. We can all have dinner together." Even Grandma smiles at that, and it starts to feel like the old days, when we were all living together and everyone was happy—or at least, it seemed that way.

"Hi, everyone." Claudia's voice sounds scratchy and far away through the speakerphone.

"How's Macro going?" Grandma asks. I roll my eyes. This is *so* not the time for small talk, and I hope Claudia will put a stop to it.

"Good, good," Claudia says. "But Lucy and I need to talk to you." She says it seriously, so Mom and Grandma look at each other like something's really wrong. Like Claudia needs a kidney and I've already decided to give it to her.

"You two give me agita, you know that?" Grandma says. "What are you troublemakers up to now?"

"Lucy, I'll talk first," Claudia says. I nod, even though she can't see me, and then giggle nervously.

"What I'm about to tell you is really all Lucy's idea. I just did some of the legwork. It's no secret what kind of situation the pharmacy is in. Times have changed. People are shopping at places that offer major discounts. I know what's been going on. And I—"

"Claudia, just get to the point," I say, staring at the veggie burger on my plate.

"Okay, okay." Claudia sighs, and it sounds loud through the phone. "One day at Earth Club, Lucy was doing some online research, and she discovered a grant Mayor Danes is offering. And she told me about it. And we've filled it out together. I've mailed it in already. All done. Nothing for you to do, so there's no way you can say no."

"What?" Grandma says. "What kind of craziness is this? Show me the grant."

"In a minute, Grams," I say. "Shh."

Claudia tells them all about the grant and about going green, and of course Mom starts flipping out. She literally stands up in her chair and starts cheering and clapping her hands.

Then she stops cheering long enough to say, "This is exactly the kind of drive and determination I always hoped you two would have. Making changes! Big changes! Thinking outside the box, and not just status quo."

"Anyway," Claudia says. "Like I said, I've already mailed it in. So there's not much you can do but thank us. We're waiting for the 'thank you' part, Grandma."

Grandma proceeds to ask us a billion and one questions. She eats a french fry every now and then, but she's only had a bite or two of her veggie burger, and it doesn't look like she's going to eat any more. She asks us how much the grant is for, when we'll get the results, and what we have to do after we get the grant.

"See, Grams," I say. "We'll have more money to put into the store this way. Plus, the publicity from the grant will bring in customers! Situation solved." I smile, dipping my finger in the ketchup on the side of my plate. "Oh, we didn't even tell you the most important part! Remember when Morrie told you guys about how you should expand?"

Grandma nods and gives me a look. "But I don't remember you being invited in on that conversation, Lucy."

I smile. "Sorry. Anyway, part of the grant involves

expanding. And we're going to expand by opening up an eco-spa. I mean, we practically have one already. With the makeup and the Relaxation Room and everything."

"Lucy, my love, I don't want to rain on your parade. But this won't solve all our problems."

"What?" Claudia and I ask at the same time.

"If we even were to get the grant, it would pay for all of the new green products and whatever eco-spa you're talking about," Grandma says to me after a sip of water. "But after that we wouldn't have enough to keep the pharmacy running. Business isn't picking up."

"But think of how well we'll do once we have the green stuff, " I say. "And the spa will bring in tons of business! We'll be back on our feet. People will shop at the pharmacy more because of all the new stuff."

At this point, I've kind of forgotten that Claudia's on speaker. She hasn't said anything in a while.

"Listen, Luce, we tried," Claudia says, finally. "Okay? The grant's already in the mail, so let's just see. I gotta go, everyone. Love you all."

As soon as Claudia hangs up, I say, "Grandma, don't you get it? Having an eco-friendly pharmacy will make us different. People will want to shop there. People want to save the earth! And the spa will be eco-friendly too!" I say, louder than I intended to. "Do you even know how many earth-friendly businesses there are?"

Grandma looks at Mom and then at me. "Lucy, I love you. But I wish you wouldn't have gotten so involved in something that wasn't really your business." Grandma's voice is monotone now; she's not even yelling. I know she's mad, because she's having a hard time looking at me.

"Grandma," I say. "What happened to faith?"

She tilts her head to the side and stares at me for a second. "Who's Faith?"

I don't respond.

"I love you for trying, Lucy. You are beautiful inside and out," Grandma says.

I bet if it were Claudia, brilliant Claudia, who'd found the grant, they'd take it more seriously. But no, because it's me, little Lucy, everyone thinks it's cute, and that's it.

I hate being twelve.

Later that night, Claudia texts me: *Don't worry, Luce. It'll be OK.*

No, it won't. The store will close. I know it.

We'll think of something else.

They won't ever take me seriously.

Chin up, Lucy. OK? ILY

ILY2

Business tip: Talk and listen to your employees. It seems simple, but it's very important.

At school on Monday, I tell Sunny about what happened when we told Mom and Grandma about the grant. "They didn't even really take it seriously," I say. "Claudia already mailed it in, but it's not even gonna make a difference."

"Sorry, Lucy." Sunny puts her arm around me. "I thought it was such a good idea."

"I did too," I say defensively. "Whatever, there's no point in talking about it now." Thinking about the grant only makes me upset. And I have other stuff going on anyway.

The eighth-grade masquerade is on Thursday, and Yamir wasn't kidding when he said he'd have kids come in so that I could do their makeup. Yamir and his friends have told me they are coming in, and so have a bunch of the eighth-grade girls. I'm not sure if they're gonna want regular makeup or costume makeup, but I guess we'll see.

"Lucy, please make sure all of the kids coming in and out are quiet, okay? I don't need these shenanigans completely disrupting the pharmacy," Grandma says to me as soon as I walk into the store after school on Thursday. "Because I do have regular customers. I do have a few of those left."

"Fine, Grams." I'm putting all of the different face paints and makeups on a display table so everyone can pick what they want. "But wait until you see how much business this brings in."

"Mmm-hmmm. Lucy, I hope you're still working hard in school and not spending every second on this makeup stuff," Grandma says, walking away from me. I swear she becomes more pessimistic every day.

School got out at one today, so I rushed over to the pharmacy to get everything ready. But I still have an hour or so before the kids start showing up for appointments. I have the worst nervous stomach. It feels like there are a billion of those little bouncy balls bouncing around my insides, and I don't know how to stop them.

At three on the dot, Yamir, Clint, Anthony, Erica Crane, and her sidekick, Marnie, walk into the store.

"Hey Luce-Juice," Yamir says. "We're ready for you to work your magic on us."

"Magic?" Erica Crane sneers. "Um, okay."

"Erica, why are you even here? You're not in eighth grade." I know that's probably not a nice way to speak to customers, but it's true. I'm just stating a fact.

"Yamir," Erica says, and smiles at him. "Tell her, please."

"Oh, Erica's going as my date," Yamir says with no emotion whatsoever.

"No one brings dates to the eighth-grade masquerade," I say.

"Well, I'm starting something new." Erica folds her arms across her chest and glares at me. "Got a problem with it? No? Okay. I didn't think so."

Yamir Ramal is bringing a date to the masquerade. I can't even believe it. What is his mother going to think?

"Lucy, you okay?" I hear Clint ask. "We decided I would go first."

"Oh, uh, yeah, I'm fine." I smile. "So what are you going as?"

"I just want dripping blood down my face. So, like, a really pale white face, with blood dripping all over it."

"I thought you guys weren't allowed to be anything violent," I say.

"Whatever. The teachers love me," Clint says. "No problemo."

After I do Clint's makeup, Yamir and Anthony tell me they

want the exact same thing. I do Anthony's pretty well, but I rush through Yamir's. It feels too awkward to be touching his face like this. I don't like it. I hate when my hand brushes against his cheek and he laughs. It wouldn't feel so weird if the other kids weren't here too, if Erica wasn't here, Erica his date. But with all of them here, I just want it to be over.

Then it's Marnie's turn, but all she wants is eye shadow, and that doesn't take very long. Thankfully, she doesn't talk much. Last and very much least, it's Erica's turn.

"What do you want, Erica?" I ask her, praying she'll just want lipstick.

"I want to look like an actress in an old movie," she starts. "Like, rosy red cheeks, light eye makeup, bright lipstick."

I start doing her makeup and feel really relieved when Yamir and the boys go to the toy section.

The bouncy-ball feeling I had before is turning into a churning, sick, nauseous feeling. And I don't know why. All of a sudden, I'm mad at Erica—really, really, really mad. And I'm mad at Yamir too.

I'm putting way too much eye shadow on Erica, and I don't really care. I hope she looks horrible. I hope people look at her and laugh. I hope Yamir changes his mind at the last minute and says he can't go with her.

"Ow, Lucy!" Erica yelps. "You're hurting me."

"Sorry," I say. I couldn't have been hurting her. I was barely even touching her. Maybe Erica will look so ugly Yamir won't even be able to look at her. But he already said he was taking a date. So he'll have to take me instead. Yeah, that'll work.

"You're all done, Erica," I say, brushing more and more bright red blush on her cheeks. "All done."

I don't understand what is going on with me right now. Why in the world do I wish that Yamir would take me to the eighth-grade masquerade? Why? This is like how Sunny described her Evan crush. It just happened to her. And it just happened to me. Just now. I like Yamir Ramal. Why is this happening? Where did this come from?

Grandma walks over to me and asks, "And what do we have here?"

"I told you. Doing makeup for the eighth-grade masquerade," I say, all matter-of-fact. "It's been great for business so far, Grams." I look over at the boys, who have each bought a bag of chips and a soda, and at Marnie, who has one of the pharmacy's red baskets filled with makeup. I'm hoping Erica will say something about how so many kids are coming to me so that I can do their makeup, but she doesn't. Instead she gets up and walks over to join Marnie.

"Lucy," Grandma groans, gently patting me on the back

as soon as Erica goes over to the others. "Please, you need to realize what the situation is. I don't want to hurt you. But you're not being realistic."

Saying nothing, I hand Grandma the forty dollars that Yamir, Clint, Marnie, and Erica put in my tip bowl.

"Lucy, keep it. Really," she says. "That money is yours."

"No, honestly, I want you to see how much this makeup business is helping the pharmacy," I plead. "Really. There's still hope, Grandma."

Grandma messes up my hair and kisses me on the forehead. "Lucy, just keep the money. Okay? Can you listen to me?"

I nod. My throat starts burning, and every time I try to swallow, it hurts. I blink and blink and blink, trying to force back tears. I wish Grandma would just listen to me. It seems like the harder I try, the less she listens.

And now I have a stupid crush on Yamir to deal with too.

32

Apply your blush in a circular motion,
with the flat side of your brush. —Laura Mercier

"Did you know Yamir went with Erica Crane to the eighth-grade masquerade? Like a date?" I ask Sunny at our lockers. Today's the last day of school before winter break, and we have to do this massive locker cleanup.

"Noooo!" Sunny gasps, throwing some empty potato chip bags into the trash can next to her. "Are you sure? I mean, I know she mentioned it that day. But then Yamir never said anything about it."

"Yeah. I'm sure. They came in yesterday for me to do their makeup." I throw a few empty iced tea bottles from my locker into the recycling bin and plop myself down on the floor in front of my locker. I'm done cleaning. "No one takes dates, you know. Did Yamir say how it went?"

Sunny shakes her head. "Erica Crane is sick," she says. "Like insane, I think."

When we get to Mr. Planzin's class for English, all of the desks are moved into a circle.

"Take a seat anywhere," Mr. Planzin says. "What we're going to do today is write each of our classmates a hope or wish we have for them for over the holiday break. Not just 'Have a Happy Hanukkah' or 'Merry Christmas.' Think about something they've been working on or struggling with, and write something based on that. And if nothing comes to mind, then write a unique wish. Like 'I hope you get extra marshmallows in your hot chocolate.' Think of it like a fortune cookie."

Mr. Planzin hands out little pieces of paper and says to write our classmates' names on them and then get started on the wishes. Some of them are easy. Like for Megan, I write, "Hope you conquer that black diamond trail in Vermont." She's an amazing skier, and she's been waiting to try that trail forever. For Cassandra I write, "Hope your grandma gets better and you get to spend a lot of time with her." Her grandma just had a hip replacement and she's in a rehab place forty minutes away. Cassandra's been sad she hasn't gotten to see her yet.

Sunny's is really easy too. I write, "Hope you keep feeling as awesome as you are."

At my locker, I look at all of the fortunes people wrote for me.

Megan wrote, "Hope you get a break from working at the pharmacy," and Cassandra wrote, "Thanks for being such an awesome friend. I hope people have the chance to be as good of a friend to you as you have been to us."

Cassandra may not be the brightest, but she's one of the nicest for sure.

Evan wrote, "Hope you get to go out for home fries at Sylvia's Diner. They're definitely better than the school tater tots you love so much."

I laugh out loud when I read that. He thinks it's crazy that I love the school tater tots, but they're so good. And he's been going on and on in Math about Sylvia's Diner. I've never even been there, even though I've lived in Old Mill my whole life and it's only a block from the pharmacy.

And Annabelle Wilson wrote, "You're going to save the world one day. So get some rest while you can." It's strange how you don't realize what some people think of you. I didn't know Annabelle Wilson had so much faith in me. I feel like I want to give her a hug now that I know.

Sunny runs up to me when I'm halfway to the front doors. "I got such good ones," she says. "I love that Mr. Planzin does this."

I nod. "It's really cool."

"Guess what?" Sunny asks as we're walking outside to the parking lot.

"What?"

"Evan's wish to me was . . ." She takes the note out of her pocket. "'Hope you have a relaxing vacation and don't need to collect any recycling that's sticky and smelly. Maybe I'll see you at Lucy's pharmacy.'"

My eyes widen, and for a minute I'm not able to say anything. It's like all the emotions that I'm feeling are circling around in my brain and my mouth hasn't figured them out yet. "Sunny!" I squeal. "Hello? He likes you!"

"He does?" she asks.

"Yes!"

Sunny smiles as wide as I've ever seen her smile. "It's totally from that concealer you gave me and the moisturizer. Seriously."

"Yeah, right." I roll my eyes at her. "Makeup doesn't change who you are. Can you just take some credit that you're awesome?"

"Maybe." She shrugs.

When Mrs. Ramal arrives, I get in the car and feel so happy that Yamir's not in the car for the ride home. He was going to Anthony's house after school today.

Now that I like him, I feel exactly the way Sunny did when she started liking Evan. I do not want to see Yamir. Not at all.

"Girls, Yamir is sleeping at Anthony's tonight," Mrs. Ramal says. "So he won't be around to bother you. Lucy, would you like to sleep over?"

I feel like Mrs. Ramal just read my mind about the whole Yamir thing. Is it so obvious that even his mother knows?

My mom says it's okay, and I sleep over at Sunny's. Mrs. Ramal bakes oatmeal-chocolate-chip cookies for us, and Mr. Ramal has a fire going in the fireplace. Sunny and I make paper fortune-tellers and ask them the same question over and over again. "Does Evan like Sunny?" When Sunny goes to the bathroom, I quickly ask it, "Will Yamir ever like Lucy?" It's just so weird to like your best friend's brother. Friends' brothers are automatically considered gross, by default. And liking one feels like a curse or an illness—something unfair that just happens to you. And besides, it's like it doesn't count or something, like it's not even a real crush.

I wish I didn't feel this way about Yamir. But I can't change it now.

I need to tell Sunny. I need to. I feel like this secret is eating me alive.

Sunny gets back from the bathroom, sits next to me on

the couch, and looks at me through squinted eyes. "Are you okay, Luce?"

See, she knows me that well. She knows something's wrong. I exhale. "Sunny, I have to tell you something," I whisper. I have to make sure her parents don't hear.

"Yeah?"

"Remember when you first started liking Evan, and you said it came out of nowhere and it just happened, and then you couldn't stop thinking about him?"

She nods.

"Well . . . I think it's happened to me too." I pause and clench my teeth. "But with Yamir."

"My brother?" she says, sounding confused.

I nod.

"Oh my God," Sunny whispers. "Oh my God!" she shouts.

"Shh!" I say. "It's so weird, I know."

"It's more than weird. It's gross." Sunny raises her eyebrows and keeps them that way. "Seriously. Do you have to like him?"

"Sunny," I say quietly. Why is she reacting like this?

"What?" she asks, all defensively.

"I'm not kidding." I fold my arms across my chest. "I like him. Like, for real."

"Can we just pretend you didn't just tell me that?" She turns away from me a little bit. "Because I was really excited for this sleepover, and now it's totally ruined."

"Fine." It's pretty unfair that I have to lie about my crush on Yamir and she gets to go on and on about Evan.

We sleep in sleeping bags in front of the fireplace, but we don't talk that much for the rest of the night. I'm tossing and turning and up so late that the fire is out before I fall asleep. This is the first time I've slept here since I realized I like Yamir. And now I feel funny.

Like, I want to go into his room and look around. I've never really been in there, never really cared at all. But now I want to know. What does he have on his shelves? Does he have clothes all over the floor? Is he a neat freak? What does he spend his time looking at?

I'm tempted to go up there, right now. Sunny and her parents have been asleep for hours. No one would know.

But I can't do it. I can't be a stalker.

Even if it is just Yamir. A boy I've known since I was five.

Beauty tip: A new lipstick can be as
exciting as a new pair of jeans.

"*Hey, Evan.*" The words come out of my mouth shaky, like some little alien got inside my brain and forced me to say them. It's the middle of winter break, and it's been pretty boring so far. Sunny and I haven't even been talking much since I told her about Yamir. She's mad at me; I know she is.

But how can she be mad at me for feeling this way? I can't help it.

Evan smiles and then walks over to me. "Hi, Lucy."

"So, are you here shopping for anything in particular?" I ask. I have no idea why I'm so nervous to talk to Evan. He's Sunny's crush, not mine. But maybe this is a chance for me to fix things between Sunny and me. If I have a great conversation with Evan, I'll have an excuse to call her, and she'll be so happy that she'll forgive me about Yamir. I rub my lips together; I wonder if I still have some of the candy cane lip-gloss on or if it wore off already.

"Yeah, my aunt's and my mom's birthday is tomorrow. They're turning forty. My mom wants to get my aunt some silly turning-forty kind of stuff." Evan laughs. "She's my mom's twin, and they always get each other the weirdest stuff."

I feel my eyes get bigger. "Your mom's a twin? I've always wanted to be a twin!"

"I think it may be a little too late for that, Lucy," Evan says, and we both start laughing.

"Oh well. You know how people always say 'nothing is impossible'? Well, I guess that's one thing that is."

"True." Evan looks around the store and stares up at the ceiling. I can't tell if he's searching for something to talk about or if he's really interested in the design of the pharmacy.

Soon Evan's mom tells him it's time to go, and I feel a little relieved since there's been an awkward silence for what seems like hours. But I'm a little depressed too, because that conversation wasn't very exciting, so I don't have much to report back to Sunny.

34

Beauty tip: In the winter, make sure to wear
moisturizing lip products to prevent chapped lips.

"So what's up with the grant?" Sunny asks
on the way to the buses after school. It's the first day back from
break, and I guess we made up, or she just got over or forgot
about my crush on Yamir, because first thing this morning she
was hugging me like she hadn't seen me in years. "You've been
silent about it."

"I told you. They think it's, like, some stupid kid idea." It's
so cold my cheeks feel like they're frozen. I can't even bear to
be outside for a minute. I hate January.

"Yeah, but what about everything else? Your makeup
stuff?"

"Me sometimes doing makeup isn't gonna be enough to
save the store. And they don't even want to talk about it."

Sunny slides into the bus seat. "Sorry, Luce."

"Yeah," I grumble under my breath. I hate to say this, but

Sunny doesn't know how to help me with this. That's why I don't talk about it with her. I'm glad she's not mad at me anymore, but I just don't feel like talking.

"Maybe your mom and grandma don't take your makeup stuff seriously because you don't advertise. You don't even have a makeup sign in the front of the store."

I laugh at that. I've never heard Sunny be so direct before.

"Maybe you need to have a more professional business," Sunny says.

"We do have a professional business," I snap. "Forget it, I don't even want to talk to you about this."

She rolls her eyes at me. "No, I mean, the makeup. Duh. Maybe you need a brochure. Or some kind of cool sign."

"Whatever, Sunny. Forget it." I really wish she'd stop giving me advice. She didn't take my advice at first when I was trying to help her with Evan, so I don't have to feel guilty about not taking her advice now. Sometimes it's better just to do stuff on your own.

"Stop being so stubborn. Yamir can help you with a brochure. He knows how to use the printer and all the design features and stuff. And maybe more people will know about it if you have that."

I don't respond. Maybe she's a little bit right, but still. She thinks she knows everything.

"It'll be cool. If you feel like people don't take you seriously, then a brochure will totally help. Your grandma will take the whole idea more seriously too. It can only help her trust your spa idea, and the grant, and everything. You know?" She looks at me. "Hello? Are you hearing me?"

"Yeah," I grumble. "Fine, ask Yamir if he'll do it." As soon as I say that, I wish I hadn't. Now that I know I like Yamir, and Sunny knows too, it's going to be so hard to be around him.

Sunny rolls her eyes again. "Sure. And maybe you can say thank you?"

"Thank you," I say to the seat in front of me, instead of to Sunny.

I know I shouldn't be taking this out on Sunny. It's obviously not her fault, and she's only trying to help. It's just that the situation is so frustrating. Like, one minute I think I've found a solution. And the next minute, it's not gonna happen.

A girl can't handle this kind of thing. It's too much stress.

Beauty tip: Fruits and vegetables are good
for the complexion.

I'm on my way to Sunny's house so Yamir can
help me with the brochure. I had to lie and tell Mom and
Grandma I had a school project to work on and that's why
I wouldn't be at the pharmacy.

I hate lying and I hate this plan, but it's really my only
option. I hate that Yamir Ramal is the one who knows
how to use his dad's fancy printer. Annoying, obnoxious
Yamir Ramal. I hate that he went with Erica Crane to the
masquerade. I hate that I like him.

Why do I have to like *him*, of all people?

And I hate that I'm even in this situation in the first
place. Why can't the store just be doing well? Sometimes
I wish I were just born into another family. It seems like
no other twelve-year-olds have the kinds of problems that
I do.

"Hello, Luce-Juice," Yamir says as Sunny and I walk up

to the house. He's been waiting for us by the front door. I have no idea why.

"*Lucy* works just fine."

Yamir grins. "Oh, but *Luce-Juice* is so much more fun." He holds the door open for Sunny and me, and we walk in. "Isn't it? I mean, come on."

I don't respond.

Sunny gives me one of her annoyed looks, and I'm not sure if she's annoyed at me or annoyed at Yamir or both. "Mom said there was pink lemonade in the fridge and chocolate-chip cookies for us on the table."

"Well, there is pink lemonade," Yamir says, looking away. "Cookies, not so much. We got out of school early, and Tony and I kinda polished off the cookies."

"Yamir! That is so unfair. Mom made them for Lucy and me. I'm calling her right now," Sunny yells at him, starting to dial her cell phone.

"Oh, Sunner. Calm yourself." He smiles at me. "I was kidding."

I shake my head at both of them. "Not to be rude or anything, Yamir, but I don't have all day."

"Luce-Juice. You know, just saying 'not to be rude or anything' doesn't excuse you for being rude."

"Okay, I'm sorry. Please, Yamir, great, awesome, righteous

Yamir Ramal, will you please help me?" I grit my teeth. I have no idea how to act around him now, so I'm just pretending nothing's changed. He's just as obnoxious as he was before, anyway.

"Surely. Please follow me into my office."

Sunny grabs the pitcher of lemonade, three glasses, the tray of cookies, and a Red Delicious apple for the two of us. We follow Yamir down the stairs into the basement office.

Sunny's basement is one of my favorite places on the entire earth. It sounds crazy, I know, but it's true. People talk about the Seven Wonders of the World—to me, Sunny's basement is the eighth.

Since the last time I was here, the yellow room got a flat-screen TV, a pool table, a jukebox, and even one of those huge gumball machines that you only see at special candy stores or amusement parks.

And there's the room we're in now: Mr. Ramal's home office. It has a few computers, a fax machine, and a big, fancy printer like the kinds they have at office-supply stores.

"Okay, why don't you tell me what you want on the brochure, and then we can try to design it together?" Yamir asks me, suddenly sounding so professional and businesslike. I have to force myself not to giggle.

"Well, I think it should list the different services I offer, like full makeup application, but sometimes people just want their eyeshadow done, or they just want skin-care tips." Sunny's smiling at me—she seems so proud. "Also, a list of beauty products and makeup that the pharmacy sells, and our hours."

After I go through all the different things I do, Yamir types them up in this fancy print-design layout. He knows how to move around all the different shapes and rearrange and make everything fit. It's really kind of amazing.

"Yamir, how do you know how to do all this?" I ask.

He gives me an obnoxious look, and I realize the Yamir I know is still there. "Well, excuse me, Luce-Juice. My father is the CEO, president, and owner of Ramal Printing, and I have helped him out a few times. For your information."

As Yamir is typing and designing and readjusting, I suddenly get very nervous. "Yamir, Sunny. Um, do your parents know you're doing this? Are you guys allowed to use all the business equipment?"

Sunny and Yamir look at each other, and then I get even more nervous. The last thing I need is for Mr. and Mrs. Ramal to find out and for me to get in trouble. Then the pharmacy would lose some of its best customers!

Sunny and Yamir keep looking at each other, not saying anything.

"What? Guys, just tell me. I don't want to do this anymore. Let's just forget it. Okay?"

Then the two of them burst out laughing. Laughing like they've never seen something funnier in their whole lives.

"What? Guys, stop. Come on."

"Lucy," Sunny groans. "Why are you such a nervous wreck all of a sudden?"

"Luce-Juice, of course they know. They love your store." Yamir goes to put his arm around me, and then pulls it away awkwardly. "And I know how to use the equipment. I do it all the time."

"Okay, okay." I smile. It's hard to believe how nice and helpful Yamir is being with this. I want to give him a hug. But that would be weird. "That's all I was asking."

Finally, hours later, I have a brochure.

It's the kind that's folded in thirds. The Ramals even have a folding machine that does all that work for you. It's really pretty too—pale pink and pale green with old-fashioned-looking writing on the front.

"Thank you so much, Yamir," I say. Yamir printed up a hundred to start with, and he even gave them to me in a Ramal Printing box so that they're easy to carry home.

"No prob," he says. "It wasn't a big deal."

I nod. "Yeah, but thanks anyway."

Sunny walks to me to the door. "Are you going to be able to walk home with that box?"

"Yeah, it's not heavy."

Sunny says, "I really think this is gonna be awesome, Luce."

I sigh. "I hope so."

36

Beauty tip: Bangs are a good solution for people with large foreheads.

Mom and Grandma aren't overly thrilled with the brochure idea. They think it's a little obnoxious and it might be taking advantage of people. But the only reason they think that is because I'm a kid.

But I'm a kid who knows how to do this stuff.

Plus, it's not like I'm forcing people to be my customers. I left a few brochures on the table in the Relaxation Room, and other than that, I'm just gonna hand them out to people.

Mom and Grandma wouldn't be happy with anything anyway. They're just in their own world of depression, and nothing will help. Every time I bring up the spa idea, and getting the grant, they just shrug at me like I'm out of my mind.

It's Saturday, so I'm hoping some of my regular customers

are going to come in. I was so excited to give everyone the brochures, I couldn't even sleep last night.

All day, I'm waiting and waiting, staring at the door, hoping to see Courtney Adner or Kristin or even Erin. Finally, around one, I see Kristin and Erin coming in.

"Hey, Lucy," Kristin says. "Erin has something to ask you."

These girls have the weirdest friendship in the world. Why can't Erin just ask me herself? "Okay," I say. Erin's staring at the floor like she's scared to look at me. I don't get it.

"So . . . I was made a bridesmaid in my cousin's wedding," she mumbles, her fingers touching her forehead like she's trying to spread out her bangs. It takes her, like, an hour just to get the words out. "And my cousin is forcing me to get my makeup done and my hair done, and I hate stuff like that." She stops talking for a second. Kristin elbows her. "So, can you, like, do my makeup? And do you do hair also?"

"Sure about the makeup," I say, all excited and jumpy inside about being able to hand her my fancy brochure. "And I can do hair, but I'm not amazing at it. I can try, and if you don't like it, you can always go somewhere else."

"Okay, cool," Erin says, turning to look at Kristin, who is jumping up and down with excitement.

"This is my brochure, so you'll know what kinds of stuff

I do, and the number's on the bottom, for you to make appointments," I tell them. Erin looks it over.

"Ooh! I want one, I want one!" Kristin sings. "Actually I want two—one for Cassandra."

I'm glad Yamir printed up a hundred, but I start to wonder if I'll need even more than that.

Kristin's still jumping up and down about Erin getting her makeup done when Courtney Adner and a few of her friends walk in. That's exactly when Kristin stops jumping up and down and tries to act all cool, reading the backs of the shampoo bottles.

"Hey, Lucy," Courtney says, flipping her hair behind her shoulders. "What's new?"

"Not much," I say. "But actually, I wanted to give you a few of these, for you and your friends and neighbors and stuff." I hand a couple of brochures to Courtney and one to each of her three friends.

"Fancy schmancy," Courtney says, and I can't really tell if she's making fun of me or not.

"Well, I wanted to be more professional," I say.

"Makes sense," one of Courtney's friends says. "Well, prom season is coming up, so you'll get a lot of business."

"Cool, thanks," I say. "Here, take a few more. Pass them out to your friends."

They take more brochures. And then another one of her friends says, "This girl is like businesswoman of the year in training." She smiles at me. Hearing that feels amazing, like I'm truly on my way to being the next Laura Mercier.

By the end of the day, I've given out about fifty brochures, and everyone has been impressed. I feel so good about this. Like I've actually done something. Like having it on paper is proof. And when I think about all the people I've helped—Courtney, Kristin, Erin, even stupid Erica Crane—I realize I've actually done something here.

And the more I think about it, the more I realize how much Yamir has helped me. But then I wonder how one day Yamir Ramal can be the most obnoxious boy on the planet, and the next he can be a super business helper and designer/printer extraordinaire.

How can that be possible?

Maybe I have been wrong about him all along. Maybe he's not even all that obnoxious. Maybe he just seems obnoxious because he's Sunny's brother.

37

Business tip: Think of new ways to advertise:
Local newspapers, bulletin boards, and
community-event calendars all work well.

It's hard to say if it's the brochure itself or just
the fact that I take myself more seriously now that I have a
brochure, but whatever it is, the past few weeks have been
so busy. It's finally March, so it's starting to warm up a little.
Maybe that's why more people want to venture out. I have
at least three appointments every Saturday, and usually one
or two on Sundays. And people even come in on Friday
nights.

Yamir had to do another printing of the brochure, and this
time he printed two hundred to be on the safe side.

All this is good. But it's not great. Deep down, I'd hoped
that with the brochure, Mom and Grandma would take me
so seriously that they'd really have hope for the grant and the
spa, but that hasn't happened. Grandma's still on the phone

with Flo and Morrie all the time. She's even cashed in a CD, whatever that means.

Still, I don't give up faith; after all, that's what Grandma has always advised. Up until now, anyway. Right this second, in the pharmacy office, she's giving me one of her "what are we going to do with you?" looks.

"Lucy, I am so proud of you. You know that, right?"

"Yeah, I know, Grams."

"Lucy, listen," she says, still giving me that look. "I'm not going to beat around the bush here. I don't want you to get your hopes up. The grant and spa thing—it's not going to work."

After that, no one says anything, not even Mom. She's sitting at the desk across the office, opening her mouth every few seconds like she has something to say, but no words come out.

"How do you know it's not going to work?" I ask, agitated. "First of all, you don't even know if we're going to get it, so it's too soon to say it won't work. And second of all, maybe a green pharmacy is exactly what we need to make money." I feel like all of the anger and frustration that's been building up inside me this whole time is finally about to bubble out all over the place, like a volcano.

"Lucy, please calm down," Grandma says. "I know this is hard for you. It's hard for all of us."

"Well, what about all the money from people buying products after I do their makeup?" I ask. "I mean, I just started that professionally, with the brochure and stuff. You haven't even given it time to really get going."

"It's not enough to save the store," Grandma says flatly. "I don't want to take any more risks. End of story."

"So, well, what are your plans? Do you even have any ideas?" I ask. Right now, I wish more than anything that Claudia were here. She'd back me up. She'd help me.

"Someone is coming to look at the store in a few weeks," Grandma says quietly. "I'll know more then."

"Selling the store is such a stupid idea! Then what are you gonna do with yourselves all day? You'll end up like Nicole Grimmey's mother, who's totally depressed because she has nothing to do!" I'm yelling, and I want to stop, but I can't. I feel like nothing I do will convince them, none of my ideas will work. I wish I didn't care about this stuff, but I do.

"Lucy, I hate to break this to you, but even with selling the store, money will still be tight. We have a mortgage on the store because we refinanced, and we still have bills to pay. We still have debts."

Mom interrupts her, "Ma, stop. She doesn't need to know this. She doesn't understand."

I can't take it anymore. I hate when they say I don't

understand. "I do understand, for your information." I stand up and walk toward the door of the office. "Forget it. I shouldn't have even bothered with anything: the makeup stuff, the Relaxation Room, the brochures. It's such a stupid waste! I could be out with my friends having fun, but instead I did all this stupid grant stuff and thought of the spa idea, and it doesn't even matter anyway."

On my way out of the office, I hear Mom and Grandma calling to me to come back, but I can't. I don't want to. I slump down on one of the couches in the Relaxation Room and bury my head in the hood of my sweatshirt.

Selling the pharmacy is the stupidest idea I've ever heard of. I mean, where will we get money to live on if we do? It's not like the money from the sale will be enough to support us the rest of our lives. And besides, what will Grandma do all day? She said herself no one's gonna hire her at her age.

I imagine her sitting alone in a rocking chair, knitting or something. I don't even know why—Grandma doesn't knit. I imagine her hair getting thinner and her skin more wrinkly, and I imagine her really skinny. Is all of Grandma's talk of selling the store just a sign that she's getting older?

The pharmacy is where my best memories come from. Like when Grandpa used to pick me up so I could sit on the counter, and he'd let me have as many cherries as I wanted, even though they were supposed to be for ice cream sundaes. And when Grandma and Grandpa would let Claudia and me come to the store after it was closed and cook us dinner on the grill as we sat on the stools and watched. Grandpa could flip pancakes and omelets perfectly; he could have been a master chef.

The pharmacy is literally my second home. I feel safe here and happy here, and it's a part of me. A big part of me. I think how I feel about it is kind of similar to the way some kids feel about the tree houses they build in the backyard, or their sleepaway camps, or their grandparents' homes.

But it's not just a part of me; it's a part of all of us. My whole family. It was a huge part of Grandpa too; he's the one who bought the store, who made it what it was for all those years. And now it's one of the only connections to Grandpa that I have.

I just don't get how Grandma's willing to simply throw all of it away.

I have to do something.

"Hi, Morrie," I half whisper into the phone after school the next day. I found his number in Grandma's address book. Grandma's next door with Mrs. Ganzi and Meredith, admiring Meredith's newly pierced ears. And Mom's at some antiwar protest in Hartford that she begged Grandma to go to. Sometimes it's like she's a kid still, begging her mom to go to things.

"Yes?" Morrie asks.

"Hi, it's Lucy Desberg," I say, trying to sound as adultlike as possible.

"Yes, Lucy?" Morrie asks. I guess he's not one for small talk.

I lean back in Grandma's desk chair, thinking of the right way to say what I'm going to say. "Remember when you talked about starting a new business? Like how we should expand?"

"Hmmm," Morrie says. "Yes, I did say that."

"I mean, like, about Gary and that money he has?"

"Yes. Mmm-hmmm. What can I do for you, Lucy?"

"Well, uh, I have an idea for a new business. And one that won't force us to close the pharmacy." I pause, waiting for him to say something, but he doesn't. "Ready to hear this?" I'm realizing something—Morrie really isn't very good at making conversation. Maybe Gary isn't either, and that's why Mom doesn't like him.

"Yes, go on," he says.

"Well, like, we can open an eco-spa. The video store next door is closed and has been for a while, and we can expand in there," I start. "And I've already been doing makeup, and I set up a Relaxation Room. And I really think—"

Morrie interrupts me. "Lucy. I see what you're saying."

I'm waiting for him to tell me why it can't happen. And I'm waiting for him to yell at me for meddling in my grandma's business. But he doesn't say anything right away. It seems like hours of silence pass. I don't know what to say.

Finally he says, "What about this grant your grandma was telling me about?"

"Oh, um, well, Claudia and I sent it in already," I say. I think it's a positive sign that Grandma mentioned the grant to him. "And part of what we had to write was how we'd expand. And we wrote about the eco-spa. But Grandma won't believe me that it'll work. And I think she's gonna sell the store before we even have the chance to see if we got the grant!" I'm out of breath from talking so fast.

"I see," he says.

Again, more silence.

"So, yeah, that's the story," I say to fill the silence. I can't think of anything else to say.

"Let me make a few calls," he says.

"Well, do you know what I mean by *eco-spa*?" I ask. I'm afraid he doesn't understand me. I'm afraid he's not taking me seriously.

"Yes, I do," he says. "Read *Business Monthly*. They're listed as one of the top-ten new business ventures. I'll be in touch, Lucy. Take care."

39

Beauty tip: Drink a lot of water for beautiful, smooth skin.

"Claudia!" I yell into the phone later that night. "Claudia, I need your help ASAP. And please don't ask me why I didn't tell you about this before I did it."

"What are you talking about?" Claudia sounds annoyed, like I've interrupted her. "And why are you yelling?"

"Okay, so you know how the pharmacy is, like, falling apart?"

Claudia groans. "Yeah, Lucy. I know," she says wearily.

"I talked to Morrie."

"The accountant?" Claudia asks, like it's completely ridiculous.

"Yeah. Remember how I told you he suggested that we start a new business?"

"Yes, about a billion times," Claudia says. "Lucy, please get to the point."

"Well, I called him. I told him about the eco-pharmacy, how we wrote it on the grant application but Grandma won't take us seriously. I told him about how I've been doing makeup anyway, and about the Relaxation Room. And then he called me back, and he wants to help us!"

"He does?"

"Yup!"

"How?"

"He wants to have his son Gary invest so that Grandma sees that this is a real business that could work."

"Okay, you're being serious right now?" Claudia asks.

"Totally serious. Gary will be a partial investor, just to start, no guarantees. He said that, like, a hundred times."

"Isn't his son that weirdo who always wants to go out with Mom?" Claudia asks.

"Yeah," I admit. "But whatever. Mom will deal."

"Does she know yet?" Claudia asks.

"Nope. Morrie and Gary are coming over next week," I say. "Can you come home? So you can be there? This is huge, Claud!"

"Luce, flights are really expensive when they're so last-minute," she says.

I guess she's right; I wish she wasn't at a school so far away. After a few seconds of silence, Claudia says, "Oh my God! I have the best idea. This summer, I'll help out at the spa. Oh, and we can hire, like, cosmetology students instead of serious professionals, so we can save some money that way."

"Good idea," I say. I'm so glad Claudia's not telling me I'm crazy.

It takes me forever to fall asleep once I go to bed. And even though I should be excited about all of this, I feel worried still.

40

Beauty tip: Try not to chew on your
lips when you're nervous.

"Mrs. Deleccio, you're going to be so proud
of me," I say first thing when Sunny and I get to Earth
Club.

"I'm always proud of you, Lucy," she says. That's the
response all teachers would give, I bet.

"Yeah, well. Guess what?"

"What?" Mrs. Deleccio replies.

"Well, first of all, I actually applied for that grant I told
you about," I say, and Mrs. Deleccio's face lights up. "My
sister helped me a little bit. And we already sent it in and
everything!" I guess I didn't need to mention that Claudia
helped me, but it would have been lying if I didn't. Still,
I wanted Mrs. Deleccio to realize I was capable of doing a
lot of it on my own.

"That's wonderful, Lucy. Really wonderful."

"And there was a part about expanding the business.

Well, I think my family's pharmacy should expand into an eco-spa!" I say.

"Wow!" is all Mrs. Deleccio says at first. Then she says, "So tell me how you thought of it. And how you're gonna do it. Tell me everything!"

I go into the whole thing about how negative Grandma's been and then about Morrie's idea about starting a new kind of business. And then about Claudia's birthday trip to the eco-spa in Chicago. And before I know it, Mrs. Deleccio is leading me up in front of the whole club.

"This is a model Earth Club member," Mrs. Deleccio says. "Lucy is proof that our work in Earth Club really relates to our everyday lives. We can do more than recycle at school. Though that's great! But we can do more. I want Lucy to be a role model for all of you!"

"Way to go, Lucy!" Yamir shouts.

"Yeah, Lucy!" Evan and his friends start chanting. "Yeah, Lucy!"

I can't help but feel amazing. To think I didn't even want to join Earth Club. Now Mrs. Deleccio says I'm a model member. And it's more than that—my work at Earth Club has done more than just help the earth. It's helped my family too.

"Hey, Sunny, want to go collect the recycling?" Evan yells across the classroom.

Sunny pops up from her chair and leaves with him. I sit back in my chair, feeling good about that too. I print out a few more Web pages from eco-spas, just so I'll be prepared when Morrie comes and we all talk to Mom and Grandma.

Beauty tip: When doing someone's makeup,
highlight their best features.

$It's$ $Saturday$, and all day I've been preoccupied.
I did a pair of twins' makeup first thing this morning,
before they had to go to temple for their bat mitzvahs. I
wasn't entirely pleased with how they came out. I mean, they
seemed to like it; they thanked me a billion times and even
left twenty-five dollars in the tip jar. But still, I know it wasn't
my best work ever.

Now I'm just sitting here in the Relaxation Room all by
myself, worrying. What if Morrie changes his mind? Or Mom
and Grandma freak out that I did this?

I'm so stressed that I'm pulling the feathers out of my down
vest. By the time this day's over, my vest will be completely
featherless and I won't be able to wear it anymore.

"Luce-Juice!" I must have fallen asleep, because I'm startled,
and my eyes pop open. Yamir is standing over me.

"Oh, um, hey." I rub my eyes and try to straighten my hair. I wonder how long I've been sleeping and why no one decided to wake me up. I hope I didn't keep anyone from coming into the Relaxation Room.

"Sleeping on the job again?" Yamir teases. "Way to go."

I roll my eyes at him. "For your information, no one is in here now. Plus, I did two makeup jobs this morning. I bet that's more than you did today."

He cracks up, tilting his head back with laughter. "Yeah, that's true. I don't work." He grins at me. "Anyway, how are we doing with the brochures?"

"Fine."

"Need any more?"

"Nope."

"Way to be friendly," Yamir says. "I don't get you. Why're you like Miss Nice one day and Miss I Hate You the next?"

"You accused me of doing a bad job," I mumble.

"I'm kidding. *Kid-ding.*" He smiles and folds his arms across his chest. "So, uh, how's business?"

"It's all right. Going okay, I guess." I sit up, and my back feels stiff and achy, probably from sleeping on the couch. "So, what's up? What are you up to today?"

Some kids at the front of the store call Yamir, and he turns around. "What? Guys, I'm back here." He faces me again and shakes his head like his friends are such a hassle. "Listen, I was wondering if you wanted to see if you can get a break. And, uh, come to the movies with me and the boys?"

I laugh. "The boys?"

"Clint and Tony."

I can't believe Yamir's actually asking me to the movies right now. Like, to go with him and his friends, not even with Sunny. "What about Erica Crane?" I ask slyly.

He rolls his eyes and juts his chin out. "Come on, Luce-Juice."

"What?" I ask, trying to be all innocent.

"I'm not going out with Erica Crane," Yamir says. "So, you in? Or not?" Now Anthony and Clint are standing next to Yamir, not saying anything, already digging into their gummy fish and sour twists.

"Nah, I really can't," I tell them. "I gotta stay here and do some work. For real. But thanks for asking."

"Loser," Yamir says. "Just kidding."

"Have fun," I yell to them as they're leaving the store.

Ever since he helped me with my brochure, Yamir's been in here at least once a week. If he comes in alone, he always pretends he's buying something really important, but usually he just gets, like, a pack of gum or something. And if he comes in with his friends, they stay for a while and request sodas from the counter. And Yamir always asks about the business, sounding like an adult, like he owns stock in it or something.

I want to go to the movies with him. I really do. I just can't handle another thing to worry about right now.

42

Beauty tip: Dab some foundation on your eyelids
for a fresh, awake look without eye shadow.

I couldn't sleep at all last night. I got so frustrated
tossing and turning that I decided go online and research
more eco-spas. I figured extra information couldn't hurt.

I can't believe today's the day. Today's the day Morrie and
Gary are going to come to the pharmacy and we're going to
sit down and tell Mom and Grandma the plan. This could be
totally awesome, or it could be the worst thing ever.

I try to keep busy. I offer some customers makeup tips.
Rearrange the Relaxation Room magazines. Organize the toy
section.

At five forty-five, I start to get antsy. They're supposed to
be here at six.

I walk over to the office, all set to barge right in, even
though the door is closed. I want to make sure Mom and
Grandma are in a good mood.

But the arguing stops me.

"Jane, I am sick of you! Sick, sick, sick. Why don't you just get another job somewhere else? I'll do fine without you." Grandma's not really a mean person, but sometimes she says really mean things. And things that don't even make sense; it was Grandma's idea that Mom go back to school to become a pharmacist and work here.

"Ma, you won't even listen to reason. You won't take anyone's advice. You think you always know better!" Mom says. "But you don't. You don't realize that our pharmacy is stuck in the 1980s. We need to make some changes!"

I don't have to crouch next to the door like usual; I bet I could be all the way across the store and still hear them.

"I don't know why you can't understand this, but I don't want your advice!" Grandma's yelling at the top of her lungs.

"I have half a mind right now to take Lucy and move out!" Mom shouts. "You're losing your mind!"

Oh God. Living alone with Mom. No Claudia. No Grandma. That would mean tofu scramble and Spanish rice every night for dinner and Mom dragging me to every rally she goes to.

"Get out, Jane." Now Grandma's talking in a normal tone of voice. "Please, get out of the office, get out of the store, and go home. I need a break from you."

"You're kicking me out right now, Ma?" Mom asks,

sounding a little pathetic. "You're kicking your only daughter out?"

I can't take the yelling anymore. And now they're going to be even more furious when they see Morrie and Gary show up.

This is my only chance.

"Can you guys please just stop yelling for one second?" I say as soon as I open the door, not even giving them a chance to continue arguing. "I have something to tell you. Something important, about the store."

"Lucy, this isn't the time," Mom says. "And frankly, I don't want you to be burdened with this. I don't even want you to be a part of this anymore! The last thing I would want is for you to end up working here when you're my age."

"Jane," Grandma says warningly. "Lucy, really, your mother is right. This isn't the time."

"It *is* the time!" I yell, louder than I've ever yelled at my mother or grandmother before. They think every moment *isn't the time*. "It *is* the time, because I have a solution!"

"Lucy, please," Mom says. "I know you want to—"

"Listen!" I say. "Just stop yelling for ten minutes. Some people are coming to see you."

"Oh, Jane, what has she gotten into now?" Grandma asks Mom. "You've been making her spend way too much time here."

I shoot Grandma a look. Why is she blaming Mom for what I do? I swear—she can find a way to blame Mom for anything. I would never tell her that because she'd be furious, but it's true. "Please. Just stop talking for a second!"

At that moment—six on the dot—Morrie and Gary walk in. We can hear them calling from the front of the store. At least they're prompt. That's one really important thing to look for in a business partner. "Hi," I say quietly, peering out from the office. They smile and come to join us.

"Oh no," I hear Mom mumble under her breath. She gives me a dirty look, but I pretend not to notice.

"Morrie?" Grandma asks. "I thought you were supposed to be in DC this week." Then she sees Gary. "Gary? What on earth—"

"Doris, Jane," Morrie starts. "I'm not sure you knew that you had a budding entrepreneur in your family. She has reached out to me. And I know this plan will make a difference to the store and will help financially, at least for now."

"Morrie, what on earth are you talking about?" Grandma asks, banging her hand on the desk. "Please, sit down and explain."

Gary and Morrie sit down, and Morrie says, "Lucy told me about all that she's been doing around here. And then about her desire to start an eco-spa. And really, it's crystal clear. It makes so much sense."

I nod with my teeth clenched, looking back and forth at Mom and Grandma. They don't look mad, really. Just confused. And a little bit exhausted.

"And Gary's your new investor," Morrie says.

"I'm thrilled about this," Gary begins. "Just thrilled. This is exactly the kind of business I wanted to get involved in. People say men don't care about spa treatments, but I do. I love the sauna. And besides, eco-friendly is right up my alley!"

"Really?" Mom yelps. "I had no idea."

"Oh yes. Always," Gary says, smiling at her.

"I still have no idea what we're talking about here," Grandma says wearily.

"We're starting an eco-spa. Right here. You're expanding into Eli Mayner's old store next door. I've already been in touch with him. I'm your business consultant. It was Lucy's idea. If the grant comes in, even better. But for now, we've got enough to start. We'll see what happens."

"So Gary's now a partial owner of this store?" Grandma asks.

"No, not exactly," Morrie says. "He's an investor."

"I like the sound of that," Mom says, smiling at Grandma. But Grandma doesn't smile back.

"Here's a binder of all my research, Grams," I say. "I'm an expert on green businesses. Mrs. Deleccio says I'm a model Earth Club member. Claudia suggested we hire cosmetology students to save money. But we'll worry about that as it gets closer to summer."

Grandma takes the binder and begins flipping through it. Her eyes bulge, and she puts her head back against the chair. "I can't believe this," she says. "I can't believe you did this."

We all sit and stare at each other for a few seconds. I guess no one really knows what to say. Then Grandma says, "Morrie, you're sure we can do this? You're my financial planner. So whatever you say, I believe—when it comes to money, anyway." She starts laughing. "You know that, right?"

Morrie nods. "Dor, would I steer you wrong?"

Grandma shakes her head. "I don't even know anymore. I guess it's worth a shot," she says under her breath.

When she says that, it feels like my skin heats up, like my hands are moving uncontrollably and everything that I had hoped and planned for might be working out.

"So, what's our next step?" Grandma asks Morrie.

"You can ask me too, you know," I say. "Next step is having Eli Mayner come in."

Grandma shakes her head. "I can't believe this, I can't believe this," she repeats, over and over again.

Beauty tip: For special occasions, wear different makeup than you wear for everyday life.

Where we live, proms happen at the end of March. It's kind of weird, but it's also a special tradition. Claudia told me that they started doing it twenty years ago, because they wanted the prom to be set apart. If they waited until June when school was ending, it would just be thrown in with graduation and graduation parties, and it wouldn't be as big of a deal.

I'm not sure why the prom is such a big deal in the first place. Isn't it like every other school dance, just with a fancier dress? I mean, yeah, it's not at the school gym. Claudia's was at the aquarium, and that's cool. But everyone gets so obsessed with the prom. All the magazines have prom specials, and all the girls freak out over dates. I just don't get it. But maybe I will when I'm old enough to go.

I probably shouldn't keep saying that the prom isn't a big deal, because it is great for me. I have tons of appointments.

And luckily, all the schools in the area have their proms on different dates, so I'm not completely booked one day and then completely free the next.

As I do everyone's makeup, I think about the spa in the back of my mind. I imagine what it's going to be like. Sometimes I forget everything I did to get where I am now, and when I remember I get this bubbly, fizzy feeling inside.

"So you're sure this tinted moisturizer is the right tone for me?" Laura Gregory asks. I'm doing her makeup, and I've been completely lost in a daydream for, like, ten minutes. She's a junior, but she's going to the senior prom with a guy from Waterside. I step back a little and look at her face. Surprisingly, despite my daydreaming, she looks very good.

"Definitely. You don't want too much tint. It's not supposed to be bronzer. It's just supposed to be a little extra color," I tell her. Then I continue to work.

After a few minutes, I say, "So tell me about the guy you're going to prom with."

"It's a little random," she says as I cover her eyelids in light silver shadow. "I'm going with this guy, but I only know him from countywide tennis, and we're not even really friends. But whatever, it'll be fun."

I smile. It seems fun to me. I bet Laura Gregory is gonna go to lots of proms.

"I had my hair done an hour ago. It still looks good?" Laura asks.

I nod.

"Next I have nails, and then I'm going home to take a nap sitting up!"

A lot of Laura Gregory's friends are going to proms with guys from different schools. And even the ones who aren't come in just to hang out. They were all in here together earlier, taking pictures all over the store, in the Relaxation Room, at the counter. It was full of people laughing and people buying things, and they all wanted to be there.

The next few weeks are so busy that Sunny and I barely even talk to each other outside of school. At our lockers in the morning, she updates me on the Evan Mass stuff, and I update her on all the makeup I've been doing and all the stories I've been hearing from the high schoolers. All the little things that had been annoying me earlier about Sunny—her negative attitude about Evan, the Yamir stuff—have just kind of melted away. I think I'm too hard on Sunny sometimes, as if in a way I expect her to be perfect. I shouldn't have been so annoyed with her about her weirdness about Evan at first. It was a completely new thing for her (for me too, I guess), and I should have been more patient.

Seeing all these high school girls has given me new insight into friendship. Best friends go through phases when they annoy each other. That's just how it is.

"So you hear about the grant pretty soon, right?" Sunny asks on our way to Math. "But do you even still need the grant?"

"Yeah, we definitely do. The grant will help us make the pharmacy green, which will make us different from other pharmacies," I say. "So we kind of needed both things to happen."

"Next year you should really join Future Business Leaders of America," Sunny tells me. "Because you're seriously on the right path. Laura Mercier started at seventeen, right?" she asks.

I nod.

"Well, you may be in business by thirteen!"

Beauty tip: Before an event, always
do your hair before your makeup.

When I get to the pharmacy after school, my first appointment is already there. Today is the last of my prom appointments, since Old Mill High School's prom is tonight and theirs is the last of any in the area. I like that. The prom I'll go to will be last in the region, and last is usually the most special.

"Lucy, Courtney Adner is waiting for you," Grandma says as soon as I walk in. Usually Grandma doesn't get too involved in my appointments, but of course she knows Courtney Adner. Ever since the hair trauma, Courtney's almost become one of the family.

"Hey, Lucy D.," she says. She's the only one who calls me that, but I like it.

"Hi, Courtney." I smile. "Are you excited for prom?"

"Yeah, I am. It's just so weird to be graduating so soon," she says.

"I know what you mean. Claudia was so sad at first. But she loves Northwestern." I smile.

She shrugs. "It'll be okay. Eventually."

"So let's get started." I dab some different powder colors on her cheeks just to get a sense of which will look the most natural, and then I try to coordinate them with the eye shadows.

"My mom is obsessed with me going to prom," Courtney says as I'm putting some powder on her chin. "She was begging to come with me when I got my makeup done, my hair done. I tried to explain to her that people go with their friends, not their moms."

"Yeah, I've noticed here that moms are obsessed when their daughters do this stuff." I step back a little to make sure her skin all looks even. I feel like Laura Mercier right now, making sure the skin is perfect before I do anything else.

"Totally," Courtney says. "So make sure you're prepared when it's your time for prom!"

After a few minutes of silence, with just the sounds of the powder brush against Courtney's cheeks, I think of something to say. "Are you and your mom close?" I ask. I'm thinking back to the fall and homecoming and Courtney screaming at her mother on the phone.

"Yeah, kinda. She's sad about me going away to school,

though." She shrugs. "But she's happy that I'm going. Happy and sad. Know what I mean?"

"Yeah, I know." I put some silver eye shadow on the top of her eyelids. "I live with my mom and grandma. So I have this on, like, two levels!"

Courtney laughs, and I go back and touch up her blush.

We're almost done when Taylor, Brooke, and Petra, Courtney's best friends, walk in, ready for their appointments.

"Hey, Lucy!" They all scream, running over to us. "Ohmigod, Court, you look amazing."

"Thanks," she says.

I ask them who they're going to prom with. Brooke and Taylor both have boyfriends from other schools, and Petra's going with a friend from Old Mill High School.

"Oh, I'm going with this kid," Courtney laughs when I ask her. "I mean, he's kind of my boyfriend. But I don't think we'll stay together when I'm at school next year. He wants to, but I don't." Courtney laughs again and shakes her head. "Lucy D., you're, like, twelve and I'm telling you all of this. How weird is that?"

I smile.

"She's twelve going on eighteen," Taylor says. "Lucy is so easy to talk to."

That's the best thing anyone could say to me. "Thanks!

Courtney, open your mouth a little bit so I can test this lipstick on you."

"Make sure it's really light, okay?" she says. "I hate bright lipstick."

"I do too. But this is light. You'll barely be able to see it."

After I'm done with Courtney's makeup, she thanks me a million times. She stays to hang out while I do the three other girls' makeup, and when they all leave, they tell me they'll definitely be back to get their makeup done for graduation.

I feel like those girls are my real customers, like the customers Grandma has. I don't just do their makeup; I really know about their lives. I didn't realize this until now, but it is what I've been hoping for all along.

45

Beauty tip: Put a little lemon juice in your hair at the
beginning of spring, and you'll have natural
highlights by the end of summer.

It's a rainy Saturday, and I'm sitting on
the windowsill inside the front of the pharmacy, eating a
cinnamon-raisin bagel with cream cheese.

"Lucy, I know you're eating breakfast, but there's a huge
stack of mail here that really needs opening," Mom says from
the office. "So when you're done, can you come open it?"

"Yeah," I grumble. It's annoying—the mail was only my
job when I didn't really have any other jobs. Now that I do
makeup and keep the Relaxation Room clean and everything,
why do I still have to open the mail? I really can't wait until
Claudia comes home for the summer so she can help out
around here too.

So I force myself to eat my bagel as slowly as possible.
I scoop some extra cream cheese off with my finger and eat

it, even though I know that's kind of disgusting. I count how many times I can chew a bite before it disappears. I'm purposely stalling, but I don't care. I hate opening the mail.

Now that all this stuff is happening with the spa, how can I possibly just go back to my old jobs around here? That just doesn't seem fair.

Plus, I have to prepare. Eli Mayner's coming in tomorrow to discuss the expansion.

Eli Mayner owned the video store next door to the pharmacy for many, many years, but the store closed last year, since everyone pretty much rents their DVDs online now. He still owns the building, though, and that's why we're trying to make a deal with him. It was sad when the store closed, but Eli's the kind of guy who just picks up and starts a new business. He bought a Web site that offers cheaper ways to rent cars and hire movers and even buy plane tickets. Grandma says he's doing very well.

I'm halfway through the mail when I come to a big white envelope. It has my name and the pharmacy's name and address printed in thick black printer letters. The return address in the left-hand corner reads MAYOR DANES'S OFFICE.

My heart starts pounding. I wasn't expecting this to come today. Part of me has forgotten about the grant, because I'm so busy thinking about the spa.

I don't want to open it; I don't want to know if it's bad news. I don't want it to ruin tomorrow with Eli Mayner.

I sit at Grandma's desk, the envelope in my hands. I can feel it getting wet from the sweat on my palms. I peer around and peek through the office door—I don't hear Mom and Grandma at all. I stand up and look around, but I don't see them either. Then, through the big front window of the pharmacy, I see them standing outside on the sidewalk talking to Mrs. Ganzi from the movie theater and Bruce from the fish market and a few other people who work at stores on this strip of Ocean Street.

I might as well find out, I tell myself. I'll open it, and if it's bad news, I'll just put it away and deal with it later. I turn the envelope over to rip it open with the letter opener.

But I don't need to open it to know the news that's inside.

Because right on the back of the envelope, it says CONGRATULATIONS in black capital letters. Underneath, it says YOU ARE A RECIPIENT OF THE OLD MILL GOING GREEN GRANT.

I sigh, the biggest sigh of relief I've probably ever sighed in my entire life. That's so nice that they put the news right there on the back of the envelope. It's really considerate—like Mayor Danes and the people at his office know how nervous people'll be when they see that letter in their stack of mail.

I take the envelope and stand it up in the keys of Grandma's computer keyboard. The back of the envelope is facing out, so the first thing Grandma will see when she gets back to the office will be CONGRATULATIONS.

46

Beauty tip: A positive attitude goes a long way when it comes to beauty and life.

"So, tell me more! Tell me more. When are you guys knocking the wall down between the pharmacy and the video store? When are you starting construction on the spa?" Sunny asks over the phone later that day. I can't stop smiling from the good news about the grant, and I also can't seem to stop talking about it. Grandma, Mom, Claudia, and now Sunny are so excited. "And are you gonna have one of those big ribbon-cutting ceremonies?"

"I don't know. The video-store guy is coming over tomorrow," I say. "But I hope we have one of those ceremonies! I want to be the one who gets to cut the ribbon."

"I bet Claudia will get to do it," Sunny says. "I feel like she'd beg for that."

"Yeah, you're right." I figure I can give Claudia her moment in the sun. She did a lot to help me. "So, you and Evan—what are you guys?" I ask Sunny, changing the subject. We've been on the phone for twenty minutes, and the whole conversation has been about me. I'm excited about the grant, but sometimes even a businesswoman needs some gossip.

"What do you mean?" Sunny asks.

I hope I'm not being too nosy asking these kinds of questions, but I really think Evan is Sunny's boyfriend. And I'm not sure if she realizes that yet. "I mean, like, are you and Evan officially together?"

"Ummm." Sunny pauses. "How would I know?"

I want to try and find a way to explain this, even though I have never had a boyfriend before. But Claudia has. And other girls in our grade have. And if you have a boyfriend, you should know. "Okay, remember when Kelly Patterson was going out with Lucas Finney?"

"Yeah," Sunny says.

"Well, remember when Kelly didn't know if they were even boyfriend and girlfriend, but she didn't really like Lucas anymore anyway and she wanted to go out with Troy Selub?"

"Yeah."

"So, like, Kelly had to ask Lucas. And Lucas said he thought they were going out. But then Kelly just broke up with him at the end of lunch that one day when they served fish tacos?"

"Oh yeah!" Sunny says.

"So you just need to ask Evan," I tell her. "Just ask if you're boyfriend and girlfriend."

"I can do that?" Sunny asks.

"Totally. When are you seeing him next?" I ask.

"I guess Earth Club next week. And you better be coming. Prom's over now."

"I wouldn't miss it."

"So what're you gonna name the spa?" Sunny asks. "I've been thinking about it, but nothing good has to come to me. It's gotta be something with *green* in it, though, especially now that you got the grant, don't you think?"

"Hmmm," I say. "You know, I haven't even really thought about it."

"Well, you've been busy," Sunny says. "But I love thinking of names. So . . . something *green*."

"Yeah." I pause to think for a second.

Sunny says, "And also something with *pink* in it, because, like, the makeup stuff, your love of anything pink. You have your Pink Lollipop lip-gloss that you love and that I'm obsessed with now too."

"Yeah, isn't that stuff amazing?" Truthfully, I'm not so worried about a name right now. I'm just glad the whole thing will happen. We could call it "Old Mill Spa" and I'd be perfectly happy.

"Well, so far we have two things for the name: *pink* and *green*."

"Okay, *pink* and *green*," I say. "Maybe I'll ask my mom. She's already looking through the magazine catalogs for environment-themed periodicals. And she started an article for the *Old Mill Observer* about our renovation."

"She's probably so proud of you." Sunny laughs. "Changing the world one Desberg at a time."

"I guess." I lean back and look at my mother sitting in the massage chair with her head back. For the first time in months, she actually looks relaxed. And for the first time in months, I actually *feel* relaxed.

"You know, 'Pink and Green' isn't such a bad name for a spa," Sunny says. "Think about it."

Beauty tip: Dab a little perfume on each
of your wrists before a special night out.

𝒴amir comes to meet me at the pharmacy at
six on the dot, just like he said he would. Sunny's at Indian
dance, so I don't need to feel weird that we're going to the
movies without her. Or that I'm going with Yamir instead
of her.

I like that Yamir's on time. And I'm not saying that
Yamir's my boyfriend or anything, because he definitely
isn't. But if he were, I'd like the fact that he's prompt. It's
an important quality for a boyfriend to have.

"What snacks should we get?" Yamir asks me, already
scouring the candy aisle.

"So you're only going to the movies with me so that I
can get us free snacks before, right?" I ask. "You're always
after that employee discount."

He gives me a look. "You're dumb."

"I am not."

"Are too," he says.

Even though I like Yamir now, things really haven't changed so much.

We pick out chocolate-covered peanuts, my favorite, and sour twists, his favorite, and then a bag of kettle corn, which we both like. And then we head over to the theater.

All throughout the movie, *Superpower Aliens 3*, I'm squirmy in my seat. It was Yamir's idea to see this movie; I couldn't care less about the *Superpower Aliens* movies. I bet there are gonna be a billion of them, and they're all going to be exactly the same. But I try as hard as I can to pay attention to what's happening on the screen. At least that way, Yamir and I will have something to talk about after the movie. And maybe next time, when I can pay better attention, when I'm used to seeing movies with Yamir, we can see a movie that we'll both like.

I'm pretty confident that there will be a next time.

Right now, we're sharing the bag of sour twists. He puts his hand in the bag to get one, and then I put my hand in the bag.

And when there's only one left, Yamir rips it in half so that we can share it. He gives me my half and then grabs my hand, pretending he's scared about the alien that's about to get killed on the screen.

Yamir Ramal is holding my hand.

But as soon as I get used to that idea, he lets go.

After the movie ends, we walk back to the pharmacy. Sunny's meeting us there when she's done with Indian dance, and we're going out for pizza with Evan, Sunny, and a few of Evan's friends. I don't know if that counts as a date or not, but it sounds fun either way.

I peek into the pharmacy window to see if Sunny and everyone else is there already. I don't see them. But I see a group of girls hanging out by the makeup section, talking and laughing, and some boys in the snack aisle.

And I see Mom and Grandma, standing arm in arm, looking into the Relaxation Room.

"I can see it now, on the pages of *Connecticut Magazine*," Yamir says, spreading his hands out in the air like he's seeing the magazine page in big letters: "Youngest Entrepreneur Ecologist in Connecticut History Saves Her Family Business and the Earth at the Same Time!"

I laugh. Yamir's probably going to grow up and be a movie producer, or maybe just write the trailers. He just has a way of making things sound good.

"What? Don't laugh. I mean it," he says.

"Okay." I shrug. "I'll take it. I hope I get to be on the cover then, and be in a fun photo shoot, and maybe also get a new wardrobe."

"Just don't forget about me when you become big and famous, okay?"

"How could I forget you?" I ask. "You'll be designing my brochures and my business cards and whatever else I need."

He grins and sits down on the sidewalk right outside the pharmacy. I'm relieved; I don't feel like going inside yet. I want to keep hanging out, just the two of us.

"Sounds good to me," he says.

I sit down next to him on the sidewalk, and he grabs my hand again. But it's different this time, different than before, at the movies.

Because this time he's holding my hand and not letting go.

And I'm not letting go either.

Acknowledgments

It may be cliéhéd, but I'll say it anyway: This is a dream come true, and I couldn't have done it without all the love and support from family and friends.

First and foremost, thank you Mom and Dad for putting up with me, for encouraging imagination, for raising me in a home full of books, and for always believing in me. I could fill up a whole bookshelf with thank-yous for the two of you.

David and Max, thank you for making me laugh, for being the best brothers and the best friends.

Bubbie, Zeyda, and Aunt Emily, thank you for the unconditional love. The three of you have always made me feel like a superstar.

Thank you to the Rosenberg *mishpacha* for always asking how the writing was going in the sweetest way possible.

Thank you, Grandpa, for the pharmacist inspiration behind this story. Thank you, Grandma, for teaching me the importance of chocolate and vanilla. I hope they have libraries and bookstores in heaven. Thank you to my beloved apricot poodle, Yoffi, for sitting next to me as I typed many pages of this story. I hope dogs can read in heaven.

Rhonda, Melanie, Margaret Ann, and everyone at the Birch Wathen Lenox School: It's a pleasure to work in such a caring and supportive environment.

Longstocking Ladies—Kathryne, Coe, Daphne, Lisa, Jenny, Caroline, and Siobhan—I am so grateful for the writing critiques and the business talk, but I am most grateful for the friendship. And of course, the retreats.

Thank you to everyone at the New School MFA Creative Writing Program—especially Sarah Weeks, Tor Seidler, and David Levithan.

Margaret, Beverly, Wes, and Janine, thank you for teaching me so much about the world of children's books.

Thanks to Susan Van Metre for all of your creative insight, to Chad W. Beckerman for the awesome design and jacket, and to everyone at Abrams for all of your hard work.

Many thank-yous to Maggie Lehrman for all the care, effort, thought, and energy you have put into this book. You are brilliant, and an A+++ editor.

Alyssa Eisner Henkin, this book would not be a book without you. It would be a manuscript saved on my hard drive. You are a dream agent, and I am forever grateful for all that you do.

Last but most certainly not least, thank you, Dave, for always saying *when* and not *if*, for asking me every single day if I'd written my daily five-page requirement, for cooking such delicious dinners, and for loving me no matter how crazy I get.

About the Author

Lisa Greenwald works in the library at the Birch Wathen Lenox School on the Upper East Side of Manhattan. She is also a recent graduate of the New School's MFA program in writing for children. She lives with her husband in Brooklyn, New York.

This book was art directed and designed by Chad W. Beckerman. The text is set in 12-point Adobe Garamond, a typeface based on those created in the sixteenth century by Claude Garamond. Garamond modeled his typefaces on ones created by Venetian printers at the end of the fifteenth century. The modern version used in this book was designed by Robert Slimbach, who studied Garamond's historic typefaces at the Plantin-Moretus Museum in Antwerp, Belgium. The display type is Hairspray.